GRAFFITI TOMBS

MATT SERAFINI

For Menahem and Yoram, the Cannon Group, Inc.

VIGILANTE

1

LEO HOLLAND SHOOTS THE PUSHER in the throat and the man with the spiked dog collar around his neck goes spinning.

Smoke drifts off Leo's gun barrel. The young man, who can't be more than nineteen, collapses into a trash pile that hasn't been collected in four weeks because every service in the city is on strike.

The alley smells like a clogged garbage disposal and Leo tries not to inhale the stench. Blood streams from the dime-sized hole in the junkie's neck. A pitter-patter down the crinkled plastic of the garbage bag pyramid. A crimson pool on the junk-strewn ground at Leo's boot tips.

Just like that, the pusher's a ghost and Leo crosses himself as he does every time. He doesn't know if this gesture is for the fallen or for what remains of his own exhausted Irish Catholic soul, though even the worst man deserves a moment of silence because everyone starts this life in innocence.

He imagines the way it must've started for this guy. Exhausted parents smiling down on a beet-red, cherubic face shivering on a cold steel scale. Mom and Dad in awe of the life they created, telling themselves this is the moment everything changes.

It could be Leo is drawing on the uncertain hopefulness in the way back of his own past, sure, but he's probably right. This bleach-blond corpse had once been the answer to someone else's problems.

GRAFFITI TOMBS

But it takes monsters to create monsters and Baby Boy here had to endure a hundred tough breaks to find death at the end of Leo's iron sights. His glassy stare is unblinking, eyes glazed over, and his face suggests the curtain got pulled wide at the very end to reveal a universe of hidden secrets he hadn't been expecting.

It doesn't have to end this way, but it always does. Leo struggles with concepts of forgiveness and mercy because the world has never shown him anything close. The world chose instead to take his own eight-year-old son away.

Tommy would've been eighteen this March.

If Leo feels anything tonight it's satisfaction, but even that is harder to gleam after a decade of hunting.

He never expected to see sixty. What's the saying? Dig two graves if it's revenge you're after? Leo was positive he was as good as dead the moment he decided to pick up a gun and that was okay with him. This all started with a death wish. Only the fates allowed him to keep on shooting, and three presidential terms later—soon to be four with Reagan cruising to reelection—he's still going.

He assumes the fates have forgotten him. That he slipped through the cracks of a world that's rotted wood, soft and flaking away, with nothing underneath save for extinction. Easy to get lost in that kind of shuffle when everyone in this hell is circling the same drain.

At the start, Leo had used a revolver. A .32 Colt Police Positive. Too paranoid about jamming to go with a semi-automatic, though after a few nights in the trenches, he learned that he was going to need more than six shots to get it done. He wasn't a marksman but a middle school teacher in Clarkstown. Leo Holland, who used to mold young minds, is now an executioner of the most wayward among them.

It's hard to live with that contradiction, but he's too much of a coward to die by his own hand and it's always a surprise when he makes it home. A senior citizen still getting the drop on good-for-nothings. Born losers who weren't even conceived when his generation took power. The world is worse today and these miscreants didn't make it that way. They're reacting to it.

There's more to do tonight. He's never been this close to the source. To what the street is calling Blood Thunder. More than a catchy name, it makes hearts explode and minds ignite. Chemical madness sending kids diving off of rooftops for the refuge of hallucinated swimming pools.

It's decimating every borough.

Morning is close and Leo is tired. The sky becomes a lighter band of black and the steam-covered street hints at headlights moving through the haze. Slow rolling taxi cabs and honking bread trucks. The first wave of New Yorkers rising to another day.

Ten years ago, Leo would never have been in this position, racing against the sun to finish a hunt. He's slower now. Has to take a moment to steady his heart while he waits for his latest casualty to stop twitching.

He should be home icing his ribs already. Ten years ago, the punk at his feet would never have landed those surprise fists to his solar plexus but bruises are forming fast and it hurts to breathe.

He tortures himself on occasion by thinking *"What if?"* as he imagines his old life playing out. In that perfect world, Leo would wake up alongside the drivers of those bread trucks to enjoy early morning coffee. Review the day's lesson plan one last time. Count the years till retirement.

This is not that world. In this one, he works part time at some fast-food dive in the Bronx because he has to keep the lights on and it's the only connection to society he's got left and has to remind himself why he still does this. He wakes up to piss four times a night and can't even have salt anymore because his ankle swells like a prize-fighter's eye and then he's limping for days on end.

In this world, there's one more pusher hiding in this dead-end alley. Leo surveys the shadows, ready to fire on any of them because he could be anywhere. The ground shifts with scurrying rats and the open dumpsters along the wall become more unbearable by the second, a cocktail of putrefied waste he tastes at the back of his throat.

Steam rises from the hatched sewer grate. Leo squints through, honing in on the sounds reverberating like a pinball.

He doesn't see the man climbing the fire escape overhead, though he hears his frantic shuffles.

And knows where to go.

2

FIVE STORIES UP, ON THE rooftop of a bakery advertising "Old-Fashioned Donuts" across a buzzing yellow signboard, crouches the man Leo hunts.

He goes by Stomper and he's scared that death has figured out where he's hiding and is climbing the fire escape to take him.

Shouldn't have messed with that girl, man, he's thinking. *Why? Why'd we have to do it?*

She was too young for this game, couldn't have been any more than fourteen. Stupid kid desperate to take a ride and too naïve to know the ticket was poison. Catnip for Nirvana, Stomper's pal who just got his ticket punched in the alley below.

Nirvana and Stomper are kids themselves. Their lawyers argue this every couple of months before some gauze-eyed judge.

"They don't know any better."

"Look at how they grew up."

"Can you blame them for having a chip on their shoulder?"

Bless the judges. They're always glad to agree. Get to feel better about themselves because they're giving today's youth second, third, and fourth chances.

Stomper is on his sixth. Seventeen years old and with a jacket longer than Johnny Wadd's cock. Track marks up and down his arms and it burns when he pisses on account of that streetwalking pussy

4

he pays for—mostly that twat Angel who insists on looking him in the eye while they fuck. He prefers her ass, but every once in a while it's nice to be nose-to-nose . . . helps him understand what it's like to be connected to another soul.

Even sleazebags dream of better lives.

Stomper thinks about that dream because the sound of death is reality. The methodical clanging of military boots ascending the black steel staircase affixed to the side of the building.

Stomper clutches a switchblade wobbling in his fist because he isn't very good at this part. Press a knife to someone's throat and he'll tell you he wears nipple clamps in church. Just don't stick him.

Occasionally, though, you find the opposite. A snake in the steel and concrete grass. Somebody who calls your bluff. Whose steely gaze is as vacant and devil-may-fuck-off as your own.

The man coming up the fire escape is like that, but far worse. Eyeballs like blazing embers.

Stomper's back is against the chimney, chuffing plumes of thick white smoke into the sky, blotting it, muting the city. All those honking horns, screaming women, angry cabbies, all that perpetual unrest drowned out and gone away.

The rooftop becomes isolated and inescapable.

Stomper glimpses an unexpected figure moving on silent footsteps around the perimeter, flashes of a forearm or a naked shoulder where the fog is thinnest. Somewhere below, the vigilante continues to climb. *Clang, clang, clang.*

Somebody else is up here with him.

He panics and pushes from cover. Toward the iron-barred door leading off this roof, except the gate is intractable and will not budge.

Something stings his cheek. A fingertip reaching out of the fog, grazing him. Cold enough to ignite a cemetery sensation where the whole world is damp and gray. The full palm of a hand stretches through the mist, landing on his shoulder with a familiar squeeze.

Stomper isn't trying to pull the gate open anymore. His fingers press against his drumming heart. No speedball has ever made him more riled than this touch, which is pulling him back in time.

"Mom," he croaks out. Hasn't thought of her in years. He's remembering the way she used to rock him to sleep with honey-tinged lullabies. So what they turned out to be the greatest lies ever sold?

Nothing is okay and never was.

The fog shifts to reveal a glistening forearm, pallid and smooth, attached to a bare shoulder and a smiling face he hasn't seen in twelve years. He can only stutter in the presence of this porcelain angel manifesting out of his most dormant memories. He's overwhelmed by all the questions he wants to ask, none more driving than *Why did you abandon me?*

She never came home from work. He was alone for days, until his helpless screams were too much for even the most indifferent tenant to ignore. Yet here she is. Just as he remembers. Right down to the yellowjacket colors of her waitress uniform covering her now, almost like his mind is projecting details onto a shadow.

Cold tears trudge down Stomper's cheeks and Mom shakes her head, a pronunciation of sadness for what has become of her baby boy. The shame he feels is worse than anything that vigilante—*clang, clang, clang*—could ever do to him.

Mom moves closer, lips pursed as she delivers a velvet "*Shhhhhh*" straight into his eardrum.

He's four years old again, soaking up the warmth of a smile he still dreams about. The last vestiges of kindness he ever knew. It's a cleansing gesture powerful enough to eradicate a lifetime of terrible choices. Tomorrow can be a new day. A new leaf. He's wanted that forever and ever.

Moms have power like no other.

An unspoken understanding passes between them. Stomper is lost in those sweltering summer nights in their closet of an apartment. The only relief was the grinding window fan, mechanized whirrs loud enough to blot the concert of domestic disturbances and sirens.

Something like an apology passes Stomper's lips. He catches another shush for his trouble. Then there's a break in the fog overhead and moonlight shines down, bright and blinding enough to vanquish his hazy reality.

Mom is gone, but the presence in front of him remains. What replaces her is something else—the undefined contours of another body. A figure formed of negative space, an outline where the swirling mist refuses to trespass.

Without Mom's touch, Stomper's pain returns. He screams, even before spotting the vigilante coming across the roof. What startles him isn't that but the sudden absence of light inside him, all of it ripped away.

Stomper's switchblade is tucked in the shadowy fist before him. A glint of cold steel in the moonglow.

Before he can process the *how* of being disarmed, the blade tears into his stomach. His body lurches forward, enabling him to glimpse his murderer's face. A bulbous eyeball popped wide. Maggots wiggling along a skeletal jawline, burrowing through the decay.

The knife cuts upward through the softness of Stomper's belly. His insides tilt, organs shifting south, vacating his body with a series of plops as they touch down on the rooftop gravel. His intestines drag him to his knees like an anchor and he stares in disbelief at the mound of organs piled there.

The blade falls atop this mush, discarded, and the vigilante is there, his cragged face looking down. His expression holds a trace of disappointment. Someone has beaten him to the punch.

Stomper's gone before his body drops sideways into the gravel. His final thoughts in that split second between life and death are of his mother.

He knows he'll never be reunited with her. He expects nothing less from this shitty world.

3

LEO HAS THE PADLOCK IN hand, rusted flakes on his fingers, but the stairwell grate is undisturbed and the fire escape is the only other way off this roof.

So where's the killer?

He walks the perimeter, gun in hand, thinking of the figure in the overcoat swallowed by shadows at the exact moment Leo glimpsed it. The strangeness of this sighting sits raw in his gut and his chest heaves with the kind of anxiety that reminds him he's alive and has witnessed something he wasn't supposed to see.

The dead man stares out on silhouetted skyscrapers bleeding into detail on the horizon and his haunted expression carries whatever secrets were made clear to him into the next life. Leo crosses himself in reflex, only there's even less certainty whose soul he's praying for now.

He stumbled across these dregs earlier tonight, both smooth-talking potential new customers like used car salesmen. They cornered a Puerto Rican girl in an MTV tee, and one of them dropped a baggie into her fist while the other forced her fingers to close around it. Think past the sale.

Kids on the town are always down for a freebie, most dealers try and hook them young, so nobody ever thinks twice about the offer. The one Leo had shot in the alley bragged to the MTV girl about his connections, suggesting she should make fast friends with his gingivitis smile. He'd give her what she needs every time she needed it.

Theirs is a particular brand of evil because Blood Thunder isn't about creating new customers. These guys don't sell. They give. Theirs is the only enterprise in history not based around profit but plague.

Leo kneels beside the corpse, nose buried in the crook of his elbow as he searches the body. It's the worst way he's seen anyone go out, dissected in a moment by a murderer that somehow vanished like mist.

In the punk's pocket sits an elongated, diamond-shaped piece of plastic with a ring attached. A single key affixed. The plastic is stamped with the words "Steinmann Hotel" and beneath it is the address: West 43rd Street. Close to Times Square.

It's where the pipeline flows. Leo may be tired, but when these pushers don't come home today, the source will be scared into moving again, and all of this will have been for nothing.

Square one is a young man's game he won't risk playing. His knees pop when he stands and he shuffles toward the stairs with a hunch in his back and a fire in his ribs. All he's thinking about is how his body can't take much more of this. He's an old man and old men should be slouching into their golden years, retirement, grandchildren, beach days and 4:30 p.m. dinner buffets.

But his best years were stolen by someone not unlike the men he fought and chased tonight. And he's been avenging that loss ever since.

STAY THE DAY

1

THE SILVER AWNING READS STEINMANN HOTEL in stenciled pink cursive across a thick, brutalist slab extending all the way to the curb.

New Yorkers shuffle beneath it without mind, the same grimly determined expression no matter the face. They press their hands to their chests to keep their collars tight, preventing the January wind from biting their bones.

Leo steps beneath the awning and the city falls away. The neutered touch of the morning sun against the gray sky is gone and he pulls open one of doors—the Steinmann, it seems, is not up to the task of employing a doorman—and so too goes the roar of city traffic, dialing all the way down to nothing as he enters the building.

Four small stairs lead into the lobby proper. Once he's at the top, Leo turns back and notes the glass on this side of the entryway is tinted, reducing the foot traffic outside to a barrage of anonymous passing shadows.

That image makes Leo think of spirits shambling through the netherworld. Whatever happens inside the Steinmann Hotel is of no concern to the rest of New York City.

Exactly as Leo wants it.

2

SOMETHING IN THE BOWELS OF the Steinmann stirs, one orange ember atop a mound of ash, activated by Leo's presence.

The hotel groans and the sound becomes a tremor vibrating through the building, shaking loose plaster off ceiling squares and prompting light fixtures across its many floors to flicker.

One ember becomes a pyre of flame as the Steinmann understands what this arrival means. It locates in Leo the very thing it craves and the doors to the Steinmann's past are flung way open. A million pent up memories rush through.

There are always echoes in the Steinmann, but the demons caged inside this man's heart are something else.

Something the hotel would like to have.

3

THE LOBBY IS AS OPPRESSIVE as the awning out front.

A low ceiling with mirrored glass. Leo looks up and finds infinity there, a contradiction because the ceiling seems to be pressing down. He feels squeezed just moving beneath it. The claustrophobia of this city replicated inside itself.

There are three elevators on the left. Each with a sliding door plated in gold. Two with "out of order" signs illegibly scribbled in red marker. Past them is a tiny alcove with a Coca-Cola machine and a Pac-Man arcade cabinet, its screen badly cracked, a wobbly image beneath it.

Leo weaves around mismatched courtesy chairs covered in cigarette burns. Water stains make abstract patterns in the faded rug.

The clerk at reception wears a bright pink blazer—an odd choice for the hotel's color—that's at least two sizes too large, giving the young man an emaciated quality. He ignores Leo, attention tuned to a magazine on his side of the counter.

Leo taps the fake gold surface and gets no response. Whatever's on those pages is engrossing. He taps the plastic again and adds a grumble.

"What?" the clerk asks with patented New York hospitality—the only city on Earth where open disdain for the customer is baked into its charm. The kid flips to the next crinkled page and continues to read.

Leo responds with a *"What else?"* gesture, arms lifting out like wings because the answer's obvious.

The clerk sighs and asks, "How long?"

"Tonight."

"Twelve dollars."

Leo reaches into his jacket pocket and counts out exact change. "I'd like to stay on a higher floor."

A record scratch as the clerk looks up. He closes his magazine and slides it into the open. Something called BRIDES. The cover is a close-up of a blond with ocean eyes. Only the slightest hint of her headdress is visible and the headline reads, "Family Planning, one doctor's advice."

"Tying the knot?" Leo asks.

"Why does the floor matter?"

Leo smiles. "I want a view."

This shouldn't be an issue but now it's a staring contest. The clerk's no older than twenty, discolored patches up one side of his face. Calcium deposits are a minefield around mismatched eyes—one hazel, the other green. He's more a patchwork collection of people than a singular person.

In fairness, his steely disconnect probably helps to jockey a place like this and there's a lopsided smile hanging off one side of his mouth as if the other half is paralyzed. He sits smirking over a joke only he knows the punchline to.

Leo waves the bills around in his first, trying to pay.

The clerk snatches the money and trades it for the same type of plastic key Leo fished off Stomper. "Sixteen will be high enough for that."

"What time is checkout?"

This garners an even more exasperated look—like nobody's ever asked before.

"Never mind," Leo says. "I'll figure it out."

He carries his key toward the elevators. The clerk slides his magazine back across the counter and starts flipping through the pages to find where he left off.

"Enjoy your stay," he says without looking, in a tone suggesting that Leo won't.

4

ONE PRESS ON THE UP arrow and the elevator gives a distorted ding. A sickly, atonal jingle suggests the car is ready to give out for good.

Inside, the arrival bell wears knuckled indentations along its rusted metal shell. Hallmarks of an aggressive city.

It's a slow ascent to floor sixteen. Vibrations shake Leo's metal fillings. He envisions the cable snapping. The ground rushing up to annihilate him. His reflection grins through the streaked mirror glass as he considers an anticlimactic demise.

How the street would love to hear it. *"The vigilante got taken out how?"*

That same defeated chime rings out as the cab comes to rest on its destination floor. The door slides halfway open, then jams, and Leo squeezes out into a darkened corridor that's no improvement on the Steinmann's lobby.

The same stained carpet beneath his weathered work boots, only up here, small, mismatched patches are spliced in. Sections that had to be cut away and replaced without the slightest regard for aesthetics.

Fresh air cannot seem to climb in the Steinmann. This floor's a laundromat, stinking of soiled and damp clothes.

On his right, the door to 1601 looks as though someone attempted to punch through it. Several fist-sized indentations have left behind jagged and splintered wood.

Almost every door is mismatched in color and style while the room numbers are displayed with different flare. Most have that tacky, stick-on mailbox lettering, while others wear brass numerals nailed crookedly into the wood.

Light fixtures are spaced all the way down the hall. Most of them hang askew, the bulbs inside long shattered. Tiny glass grinds litter the floor, mixed in with those plaster flakes that shake down off the ceiling whenever vibrations catch the building just right.

Only the occasional lamp still functions. And the occasional lamp only functions occasionally, bathing the hall in a sporadic and jaundiced glow. Leo finds himself stepping around these yellow pools, something vaguely threatening about the sickly sodium color they create.

He resists the urge to unholster his Baretta on the off chance the Steinmann really is a hotel and not just the biggest flophouse in the city. There's no reason to scare Times Square tourists half to death, though if they're staying here, they're already terrified.

Up ahead, the path breaks hard left and hard right. A fork in the road to the rest of the rooms. A figure rushes across the opening and the nearest wall sconce flickers so the person stays plugged into the shadows. The unexpected appearance startles Leo's approach, but the person is gone in a flash and once the space ahead is vacant, the hesitant light fixture resumes its ambivalent glow.

Directly beneath that bracket, someone has spraypainted the words FEED THE BONEFREEK in a runny brown color.

Leo's hand slithers beneath his jacket to touch the Baretta grip. He braces for what he expects might follow—more punks like Nirvana and Stomper about to come flooding out in ambush. Word of his arrival has surely traveled through this place by now.

Only it's quiet as he reaches the fork in the hall and there's a crooked sign nailed into the wallpaper. A piece of sheet metal that says room 1620 is to his left. Last door on the right.

That's where he goes.

5

ROOM 1620 HAS A DEEP groove carved into the jamb beside the doorknob. Someone tried to jimmy their way inside and was probably thwarted by the chain lock.

Leo makes sure to fasten that before doing anything else.

And then he's on to the unmade bed. Piss yellow sheets tangled up in knots. The headboard, unfastened with small nails poking out of the back, pointed tips dusted in sheetrock. Outlets crackle with the constant threat of electrocution. A nest of wires spills from an opening in the corner where the wall looks to have been chiseled away, either by hungry rodents or desperate junkies.

The room smells like its condition. Raw and acrid like every city slaughterhouse. The closet reeks of mold and the only item inside is a child's dinosaur plush that's been sliced open, white fluff splayed across the shelving.

High humidity is everywhere, seeping into Leo's pores, making him feel sluggish. He remembers he's been awake for twenty-four hours. It's not that he wants to sleep in here, it's that his body will shut down if he doesn't.

He gets on one knee and pushes the mattress off the box spring. Faded crimson stains. Murder? Bed bugs? Battered victims resting their heads?

All of the above, he thinks. All of it, a dealbreaker.

GRAFFITI TOMBS

He'll make do with the particle board chair in the corner. About as comfortable as a bed of nails and as filthy as the rest of this place, but at least the worst of it is hidden inside its dark forest fabric.

The Baretta 92S is tucked inside his fist and pointed at the door and Leo finds confidence in the pistol's factory gloss blue finish. They've faced some shit, him and this gun, and the Baretta always gets him through.

He closes his eyes. There's nothing in earshot save for the current of electricity zipping along faltering wires. No footsteps or voices drifting through wafer thin walls. No distant elevator dings or closing doors. Even the city is unusually quiet in here, as if everything is afraid of roiling the Steinmann.

In a perfect world, the men he's hunting would come to him and this would be over with a few more gunshots. It's never been a perfect world. Nor an easy one.

What bothers Leo is the steadily mounting urge to flee. He is not often attuned to his emotions, preferring instead to drown them inside his subconscious, but fear spreads like a virus and this is discomfort he's never felt. It's been like this since passing beneath the mirror of that lobby.

And yet, there's work to consider. The pipeline is higher up. Room 2407, according to Stomper's key. The way the clerk at the front desk had balked at Leo's request for a higher floor is evidence too of being on the right track.

He finds weary sleep before he realizes it. Thoughts and dreams often spread together like butter and jam on toast, and it's here Kimberly always crawls to the forefront of his insentient thoughts. Today is no different. Jade green eyes framed by trembling auburn curls as she shakes her head. Disappointment, like always.

Leo hates to think of her. It isn't guilt, exactly—her death couldn't have been prevented. But he knows Kimberly's spirit is still out there, weeping over what he's become. She likes to remind him of that when he sleeps.

Her soul is as tortured now as her body had been, and she's watching helplessly as her husband sags toward the edge. Hatred spinning him endlessly like some hamster in a wheel. It's not that Leo is unable to move on. It's that he doesn't want to. There's order in what he does, and the world needs it.

Cops don't stick their necks out anymore. Only time he sees them is when they crash the fast-food place he jockeys. Except they don't ever want to pay. They want to negotiate for free food. Heroes owed and all that.

Leo wants what he had. Kimberly and Tommy. He knows he's squandering his life. That this is all powered by some desperate daydream where he one day catches up to his family's executioner and stuffs this Baretta down his throat to demand an answer to the question he's always asking.

Why?

Leo died that day alongside his family, clipped right in the soul. It's just that it takes longer for a cosmic gut shot to kill you and he's still bleeding out.

He dreams he's standing beside himself, frowning over his body as he watches it recharge. His rippling jowls are a disgusting sight, the frailty settling into his features. There's a *tsk* somewhere beside him.

"You got old," Kimberly says, halfway between delight and surprise.

Leo's heart thumps. This is new. While he always sees Kimberly when he sleeps, she never has anything to say. This is a more animated presence that makes him feel small and guilty because there's no way to justify these last ten years. The things he's done. He's a caveman acting on primitive instinct, and though he refuses to chide himself, that conclusion is never far away.

"Leave," Kimberly says and suddenly her words are echoes from the distant end of a far-flung hallway. "The gun. The knife. And the hotel."

"Wake up," Leo shouts, still outside of himself, speaking to the elderly slump in the chair, attempting to will his own eyes open and make this nightmare go away. Nothing's worse than knowing he's disappointed the only woman he's ever loved.

"Next time," Kimberly says, "it will not be me."

And then his eyes pop open and Leo is back inside his own head and the room is darker. Drawn blinds no longer hold back the light. He yawns and sits upright. His spine feels permanently curved and it takes tremendous effort to stand. His body hurts like hell, front and back, especially when he breathes.

Kimberly has forced more memories to come calling.

His loafers echoing on cellar steps, descending into the city morgue.

He remembers how he begged God to strike him dead before reaching the bottom. *Please, don't make me look at the body of my eight-year-*

old son. It's impossible for an Irish Catholic to reconcile a God who'd force a man to do that.

Life is mostly shards. Image fragments littering the mind like broken glass. That's what Leo remembers. The blood on the autopsy table. The kid's personal belongings—two army men, one green, the other tan—dumped into plastic baggies. The attendant in the white coat with overgrown fingernails. The way he pulled the sheet back and looked away, mumbling, "Sorry, buddy."

Leo paces, trying to understand what just happened. How his dead wife was speaking to him. If it wasn't her, he's lost his mind and that's a more frightening thought. Leo alone in a creaking wheelchair, the only light left in his world coming through a window in the dementia wing of some state-run mental hospital.

Life never ends well because it always has to end.

He checks around, opening the closet, then closing it. He's as alone in here as he ever was.

Why are you still doing this? he wonders, except it's a question he never asks himself.

The world is always asking, though. Each time one of Leo's victims—rapists, muggers, murderers, all—hits the slab, the world asks. The press debates his exploits. The mayor condemns them. The police commissioner calls him a "low life" on the nightly news while patrolmen and detectives, well . . . they love the vigilante when they're not on strike and probably more so now that they are.

Never once has Leo felt the urge to justify himself, mostly because there's nobody to justify himself to. The doubt weighing him down now is something new, just like the fear. Two sensations planted inside of him, growing like garden weeds. He feels weaker now because of them, less capable.

Leo stops to regard his reflection in the full body mirror on the wall. Fractured glass with spider web cracks down its length. Oily streaks bleed from each fissure, separate shards producing a dozen versions of Leo.

Most are variations on the ruthless killer he's become, some younger, others older, wielding different weapons while clothed in alternate fashions.

Another is the old science teacher in a turtleneck, salt and pepper hair and a patient, reassuring smile.

One reflection finds Leo with that trusty Baretta to his temple and that likeness grows inside the glass, pushing aside the others until it's the only visage there. Then the question returns to assail him again. *Why are you doing this?*

Unexpected laughter breaks the spell of the moment and Leo is almost grateful the bathroom door is squeaking, shimmering eyes lifting out of the darkness.

Shadows peel off the exaggerated face there to reveal a Coney Island funhouse abstraction. A pale face with a watermelon smile stretched cheek-to-cheek and nose-to-chin. A grin usually indicates humor, but the eyes here are the opposite. Vertically stretched beyond the contours of any natural appearance.

Pain and anguish in the abstract.

Leo's boot tip shoves the door all the way open and the visitor dissipates in this simple shift of light. The tiny washroom, now empty save for the sink brimming with ooze. Tarred ripples cross the surface.

He's seen enough of what he thinks is his brain on the fritz, and steps into the hall to clear his head.

Another sheet metal sign hangs there. He's certain it hadn't been here on the way in. It's written in the same illegible cursive as on those elevators below. A hasty felt pen scrawl that reads: PROHIBITED FOR HOSTEL GUESTS TO GO TO ANY OTHER FLOOR.

Which is too bad. That's precisely where Leo is going.

TAKE SHELTER

1

THE SHIRTLESS MAN IN THE doorway looks at Angela like he's about to crack her head open.

Her body wants to take the instinctive step back, but she stands her ground and presses the manilla folder against her chest.

The shirtless man interprets this as a display of weakness and is emboldened into the hall, whiskey-glazed eyes narrowing.

"You're the social worker?"

"Um—"

"They've been threatening to send you for months."

"You're . . .?" The names in Angela's head vanish. She flips open the file, cursing herself for buckling beneath the pressure. She had this family committed to memory on the cab ride over.

"Nice," he growls.

His name's there in faded type print. Gerald Dorn. A sheet appended with a paperclip indicates several arrests, various assaults and robberies dating back to the mid-70s.

Kind of guy who should never have started a family. The only kind of guy her line of work introduces her to.

"Is Peter in there?" Angela lifts onto her toes to see into the room just over Gerald's bare shoulder.

He recognizes what she's doing and straightens and leans to block her view. "You can't show up whenever you feel like it."

"We can and—"

"You need a warrant."

"What for?" she asks. "This is a check-in."

"Check the whole fuckin' floor then."

Several of the surrounding doors are open and young faces peer out. Nervous chatter pinballs through the hall and is underscored by the innocuous blather-gab of toddlers inside the rooms.

"Peter is assigned to me," Angela says. "These families might, um, have social workers of their own."

Gerald's nostrils flare. Angela imagines the urges folding over his mind. She's never one to assign evil intentions but is battling the pervasive urge to retreat. Her hand slips inside her double-knit cardigan, fingers sheathing the brass knuckles there.

No guarantee this would stop a monster of Gerald's stature, but she won't make it easy for him.

"Peter's gone," he whispers and there's a quiet admission of guilt in his words.

It's late afternoon and if the boy isn't home from school, Gerald would've said that. What he said was *gone.*

"Well then," Angela says, "we have a problem."

Gerald's face goes cold, all semblance of civility flushes from his cheeks as he takes Angela by her shoulders and shoves her, the small of her back striking the opposite doorknob. He holds her in place. She cries out as every door in the hall slams in unison, followed by the sound of bolt chains slotting into locks.

Trouble is like clockwork around here.

"You stick us in this shithole and expect it to work out," he snarls.

"I didn't . . ." Angela swallows the rest of that response as her mind flashes on her training. Never get defensive. This isn't an argument where Gerald is concerned. It's reality and nothing she can say will change that.

"Some shelter!" Gerald shouts. "If I had my family stashed in an apartment half this bad, they'd take my fucking kid. But the state decides this is okay and so we've got the privilege of living like dogs."

"You're right. It isn't fair."

His palms slide down her arms and fall to his sides as the light beside them flickers, throwing Gerald into strobe. Appearing and disappearing shadows create sinister expressions on the canvas of his face, externalizing his conflict—to beat or not to beat this bitch?

Angela's fingers close into a brass fist inside her pocket. She's thinking, *Can I smash his nose to jelly and still make it out of here alive?*

"My past is the problem?" he says.

"What I meant to say is, if Peter is no longer at this residence—"

"You want to see Peter, you gotta leave the city. Wife took him to her sister's place in Nyack. I ain't allowed to go anywhere near it. That's the condition."

"I understand."

"People aren't allowed to change, you know that? A real fuckin' problem in this world."

"I know they can."

Gerald rejects this optimism with a shake of his head. Philosophy is for grad papers and dinner parties. The last thing this man wants is a pep talk. His world is in shambles and the woman who cannot recall his name without checking her file isn't going to be the one to reach him.

He turns back toward the darkened maw of his room. A mouse scurries out from between his legs and goes zigzagging down the hall.

"There is help," Angela says, hard knuckles sliding off her fingers. "If that's something you want." She can't leave it like this. The bleeding heart inside her still has some blood in the chamber. If there's a chance of getting through . . .

She knows too well what it's like to be in a dark place.

"Gerald, I could always—"

"You're paid to care." This is a violent scoff from over his shoulder. "A different kind of whore is all you are."

Angela thinks about presenting the pay stub in her pocket to show just how little the state of New York pays her to care. But that's her insecurity rising.

She stands there feeling small and musters the courage to ask, "Why'd they leave?"

His answer takes the form of laughter. He spins and Angela thinks he's gearing up to respond with his fist. Instead, the door flies toward her face with a slam and she's staring at reflective mailbox lettering that reads: 306.

2

GERALD KNOWS HE'S DONE THE right thing. Never talk to The Man, especially not when The Man is some bitch looking to make things worse.

What Gerald doesn't know is that things in the Steinmann have never been worse. Until now it was all strange noises. A suspicion someone was hiding inside the shadows of an empty room. Occasionally there were distended voices calling out from the hallway. Those are louder now.

He's sitting on the edge of the bed, head in hands.

"You'll never see them again," the voice underneath the box spring tells him with a cackling glee. "She'll find another man and he'll be the one who teaches your boy how to shoot and shave."

Gerald ignores this. He's used to hearing this asshole and decided a while back that he's losing his mind.

He wishes he had beaten that bitch black and blue for the way she made him feel. Make this shitty state pay for what it's done to his family. At least Marlene had the good sense to take the boy and run. But she's got options. Family and friends. For him, it's winter in the city and these four walls are still better than freezing to death beneath a cardboard box.

"Lie down," the voice suggests, still gleeful but now with the chumminess of a childhood friend. "You're tired."

Gerald's always tired these days.

The room encourages this. It's pitch black. Shades down. He doesn't remember drawing them.

He falls onto the mattress with his arms stretched overhead. Fingertips tap the headboard.

He closes his eyes and thinks about life. How there never was any way to get ahead. This city is nothing but January wind, even in the summer. It chaps you to the bone. What hurts the most is the way Peter looks at him without judgment. Gerald is still just Dad in his son's eyes. A hero. He never thought he'd know unconditional love, but for a second, this monster had been allowed to become a man.

And he loved it.

But this hotel is hell on earth and it's delighted to take him apart, piece by piece. Gerald hears his life pinballing around the room. Gunshots. Switchblades. Terrified faces, screaming victims. Regrets he tries to put behind him, but 306 is his own personal purgatory and there's never any absolution.

Unless you're pure, you gotta pay.

Gerald feels as though he's dissolving, energies trickling down the bedsheet to feed the cackling voice nesting beneath. Whatever's down there shuffles excitedly and this motion prompts him back to consciousness.

He opens his exhausted eyes and lifts his hand. It's lighter now. Wetter. Through the blur he sees skeletal fingers wiggling and realizes it's more than just his energy dissolving.

Good, he thinks with one final yawn before sleep comes with the blanket of relief he's grateful to have. The only time anyone has shown him true mercy.

There is no waking up again.

3

ANGELA CATCHES HER BREATH AND fishes a pen from the cross-body side satchel slung over one shoulder. She scribbles a few words in the file: "Family in Nyack."

Easy enough to check.

At least poor Peter is in a better situation. So is Angela now that she gets to leave the Steinmann before dark, use her time in the cab to prepare for tomorrow's check-in—a single mother in the Bronx whose daughter has Batten Disease and loses consciousness every day because of it.

She intends to report the Steinmann Hotel. A true blight. Homeless families occupy the first three floors and their conditions are suboptimal. Whoever owns this place surely collects subsidies from the city. Money in their pocket that is certainly not flowing back into the hotel.

Sometimes, Angela obsesses over circumstances she cannot change. To the point where she loses sleep, fixating on the callous ways politicians accept these "realities" as problems without solutions.

They don't care. Nobody above Angela's pay grade wants to hear what she has to say about the field. Poverty doesn't have to be the norm, but on her most cynical days she feels like those in power rely on it to be an evergreen problem. Can't maintain power if you actually solve anything.

Angela walks back the way she came and the only path forward is a left turn she doesn't remember making. To her memory, it was a straight shot from the elevator.

It is possible she wasn't thinking straight, too focused on the uncomfortable task at hand. Barging in on a struggling family is never easy, and though she works hard to dispel judgment, her very presence implies their inability to properly care for their child or children and so it's a balance she's always mindful of striking.

Her footsteps become squishes as she swings the left and starts down the phantom hallway, water oozing out of the carpet. The hall then breaks to the right where it's another identical corridor of doors.

I definitely missed a turn, she thinks. No chance she would've wound through this many passageways without noting the route. She turns back because it's time to retrace her steps but pauses. The door beside her is unmarked. No room number, no sign to signify its purpose.

Same for the door across the way. And every other door now that she's looking. She starts back the way she came and everything is blank and featureless and she's wondering, *Did I not notice these?*

A disturbing realization as she winds back to what she believes is the starting hallway. The spot that had been Gerald's door. Only it is also blank and she knows damn well there had been reflective numbers here just prior to knocking. Numbers that spelled out 306. Now, she's staring at a naked slab of dented wood.

"I'm all turned around," Angela mumbles, intending to appease her rationale amidst swelling panic, though her words own a hesitation that suggests she does not believe her own futile offering.

Everything in the hotel has grown silent. She imagines mothers shushing their children behind each of these doors as if the quiet is some big joke. Prank the social worker. Maybe Angela is desperate for an explanation, but she's running out of possibilities as fast as her brain can present them.

She knocks on Gerald's door.

With her ear to wood, there isn't so much as a rustle. Angela crosses the hall and tries another room, knuckles falling, discovering the same unnatural stillness. She moves further down the corridor, knocking and asking "Hello?" each time.

The quiet is overpowering. The absence of noise where there should be plenty. It's not the sudden drought of children's voices or the dearth of screaming infants, though the coordination of both does defy logic. For Angela it's the realization that this cannot be co-ordinated, and what's at play here is something both sinister and un-explainable.

She steps to another door and knocks. A quick and obligatory thump comes back in response, mimicking her with perfect accuracy.

Angela yelps. She's attempting to form a question when another knock comes from elsewhere. And then another from the far end of the hall, and a few more, traveling up and down the corridor in quick succession. A concert of strange, percussive patterns intended to un-settle her.

This ignites Angela's flight response and she's off, running like a frightened animal, the carpet squishing beneath her, amplifying her escape as every door she passes knocks, clocking her presence.

Terror drives her body along with the realization this hallway has no end. It twists one way, and then another in defiance of geography.

Angela considers her options:

Kick down one of these doors and get out through a window.

Pull the fire alarm . . . Wait, where are the fire alarms? She doesn't see any.

Fine, scream for help. Yeah, that always works out well in this city.

Her thoughts dissolve as quickly as they arrive. Whatever's hap-pening, she suddenly understands why Gerald had declined to answer her question. It's obvious now why his wife and child fled.

They were the smart ones.

Around the next corner Angela finds the elevator. She runs to it as though it's a mirage. Palms land on dented metal doors, touching it to confirm it's real.

Her finger stabs the down button and she gasps as its light clicks on. The grinding mechanism kicks into place somewhere overhead and the knocks cease, as if startled by the elevator's grumble.

"Come on!" She's tapping the doors as distant splashes sting her eardrums. Footsteps from back the way she came. Slow and cautious but getting faster.

She doesn't want to meet whoever's coming.

"Hurry," she whimpers, grinding her teeth as the elevator de-scends without urgency.

The approaching footfalls are faster now.

Over her shoulder, a shadow comes sweeping along the wall, en-veloping the light sconces in its path, prompting the bulbs to burst in alarmed response to being swallowed by the ever- expanding darkness.

Angela spins all the way around, back pressed against the doors. Her fingertips become pins and needles. None of this can be explained, though for some imbecilic reason, she has a vision of herself in her supervisor's office tomorrow morning, attempting to try.

You'll be lucky to live that long.

The elevator doors part with unexpected quickness and Angela tumbles backward into the shaft. Only there's no car inside to catch her and she's suddenly in freefall, screaming as her body plunges through the dark.

In the fleeting light above, a shadow peers over the edge, watching her fall all the way down.

UP IN HELL

1

THE TWENTY-FIRST FLOOR SUFFERS from the same abundance of blight as sixteen, with the addition of an oversized rats' nest tucked into the corner beside a leaning ashtray stand as soon as Leo steps off the elevator.

A scream at the far end of the dim hall startles the electricity and the lights tremble, off and on, off and on.

Leo moves toward the sound of irritated knocks. Typical ambiance in most hotels, but jarringly out of place among the urban detritus, which has come to be the Steinmann's defining characteristic.

He brushes along the wall until he's at the corner, peering around, finding something surprisingly mundane.

A young man in employee colors stands beside a brass cart of poorly folded bathroom towels, no older than nineteen. Hispanic, with a thin moustache that maybe ages him north of twenty but does not mask his otherwise cherubic features.

"Hey, buddy," the kid says, rapping on the wobbly door. "Already told you, no one's supposed to be in there."

A guttural scream detonates in their ears as if in response. More than some anguished junkie in withdrawal, the noise bends the air, placing mounting pressure on Leo's eardrums. Whatever's happening in that room propels Leo out of cover.

The kid notices him and throws his hands up. "Hey, man. Come

39

off it, alright? I just work here."

Leo realizes he's got his Baretta in hand, provoking this reaction. He has no recollection of unholstering it, but that scream has shaken his nerves loose. Whatever's in there is so much worse than some fix freak.

"Oh," Leo says and lowers his weapon to the floor to deescalate the tension. "I heard the scream and thought there might be a problem."

The kid looks from Leo to the door and back to Leo, guesses he believes that, then shakes his head and returns to his cart. "Whatever. Close to quitting time."

Leo blocks his path, attention anchored to the door, afraid of what might come through it. "You really work here?"

"What tipped you off?"

"That nobody seems to work here."

"It ain't that bad."

The brass nameplate pinned to the kid's chest says *Ruben* and Leo tells him, "You ought to have higher standards." He feels equipped to speak on this since he's the night manager of a joint called Dickie's that pays $3.35 an hour and gets robbed once a month by desperate assholes with broken off broomsticks sharpened into poke 'ems.

One of these nights, Leo is going to figure out a way to ice them without tipping off his half-staffed night crew that he's the city's most famous resident—the man they're always praying will wander by and do the right thing.

"Psh," Ruben says and it's a fair point. Kid's got a life story Leo doesn't know. "Forget it, man," he adds, zero desire to explain himself to a stranger. "I didn't see shit and I know even less."

"Who's in this room?"

"Supposed to be no one."

"Room's empty?"

"Whole floor's empty."

"Why?"

"Hotel don't need all of 'em."

"You still change the towels?"

"Every couple of months."

"This floor is as high as the elevator goes," Leo says. He slides Stomper's key from his pocket and dangles it between his fingers. "I had a friend staying up on twenty-four."

"Psh," Ruben says again. "When was that? 1952?"

"A few months ago."

"Sure." Ruben's looking like he can't make heads or tails of this guy. "You a cop?"

"No."

"I don't want to get involved."

"Told you I'm no cop."

"That's why I don't want to get involved."

"This key says—"

"Please, man," Ruben pleads. "I need this job, okay? My pops got a bad injury on the job site, can't work no more. I gotta earn—"

"So earn. I only want to know what's going on up there."

"Hotel's got ten active floors . . . not counting the first three. Those were converted into a homeless shelter last year."

"So four through fourteen are active?"

"Any higher and it's a ghost town." Ruben taps his cart. "Though we do rotate the linen. We're not savages. Guess management figures the hard times ain't gonna last forever."

Leo can wager a guess as to why they placed him on sixteen. Far away from any legitimate guests who may be checked in. He was made the moment he walked in. A problem to be fixed. "Tell me about the guy working the front desk."

"Don't even know who's on today. I didn't look."

"Okay, then, tell me what's up there?"

"Your funeral." Ruben side-steps Leo to survey the central hallway. Makes sure nobody else is in earshot. The gesture doesn't seem performative to Leo, meaning this isn't some trick at his expense. The kid's paranoid, chewing his lip as he considers things. "Look, the north elevator goes all the way up. That's the one you want and you gotta pick it up outside the employee lounge. On two."

"I'll just take the stairs."

Ruben shakes his head. "Trust me on that."

"So you do know something."

"I know nobody's allowed to go any higher. Don't know who's up there, but I hear he'll put your balls in a grinder if you wanna go ice climbing."

For a minute, that's the end of the conversation. Only Ruben's watching Leo like he's got one more thing to tell him, finally muttering "*Shit*" beneath his breath.

"Something else, okay?" He whispers like he's trying to keep the walls from hearing this next part. "We cut outta here before dark."

He touches his pink coat to affirm he's talking about employees. "Everyone except front desk. Ain't a good idea to be messing around on these floors after that."

"I'm not helpless."

Ruben groans because Leo doesn't get it.

Except . . . Leo *does* get it and isn't about to indulge Ruben on topics of ghosts and goblins because conversation makes those things real and adds validity to the fear that's eating him alive.

Part of Leo has intuited the belt-coated figure on the rooftop, the thing that had slashed Stomper open, had done so to try and protect the Steinmann. To prevent Leo from finding his way here. Only those forces couldn't count on the punk carrying a hotel key in his pocket and now Leo has inherited its fury.

"Don't mess around in here, old man," Ruben says. "Get into trouble and nobody is coming to help you."

"Story of my life."

"I hear that."

Another scream from the room, louder this time. Ruben pushes his cart around the corner and picks up the pace.

Leo listens to those squeaking wheels as the kid makes a beeline for the punch clock and he wishes he was going with him.

2

LEO STANDS WITH HIS BARETTA thinking it could be the man he's hunting tucked inside, though luck has never been so kind.

His foot sails toward the knob, knocking the door off its hinges, a slab of rotted wood skidding across fresh cleaned carpet.

He stares into the dark, blinking at what's inside. An unexpected interior.

The room is brand new. A crisp and wrinkle-free bed looks comfortable and there's a tube radio on the dresser, a circular glow emanating from the center dial where Bing Crosby sings "Just One More Chance."

Leo crosses into fresh air, stunned. Another item for the long list of things failing to add up with the Steinmann. His body chemistry is at a rolling boil and won't stop bubbling until he gets out, just as Kimberly—*Christ, how could that have been Kimberly?*—suggested. But Leo has never failed a hunt and won't now.

The layout of the room resembles his own dive several floors below. The same basic blueprint, only this dresser has a straight-from-the-factory look. A glossy finish. Wood that hasn't yet warped. Hasn't yet become engraved with every slang obscenity thrown around over the last fifty years.

Pressure builds at the base of Leo's neck. The feeling of a hand crawls up the back of his head, slips beneath his skin, frozen fingers

43

closing on the round of his skull where agony suddenly strikes every part of his body.

Leo screams out, voice full of static, and goes down on one knee. The Baretta thuds to the carpet.

A parade of silhouettes swarms the room, flashes of tenebrous bodies holding only vague details—the Steinmann manifesting an army of long-faded memories. Shadows writhe together atop unmolested bedsheets. Blank bodies slump into the accent chair. Figures march to and from the bathroom.

These voices are disembodied, combining into one indecipherable bleat.

Leo's eyes feel ready to burst. He cries out and the silhouettes break from their longstanding routines as if startled by Leo's corporeal presence, converging on him like a pack of rabid dogs or curious children. A cadre of shadows closes in from all angles because this one's alive, and they've just gotta see it.

Garbled voices create one anguished roar. It hurts like hell to hear. The Baretta is halfway beneath the bed and Leo is thinking about his reflection in the broken mirror. The gun pressed to his temple.

Go on, the voices tempt, slightly out of cadence, creating a lingering hall of echoes. *Go on, go on, go on . . .*

Leo fights to his knees and the shadows lurch away in retreat, this show of defiance completely unexpected. Leo screams again and the desperation in his throat is familiar. He's heard it before.

A knock on the door comes in response.

Leo looks back and the door to the room is somehow slotted inside its jamb. Hinges attached.

"*Hey, buddy, already told you, no one's supposed to be in there.*" Ruben repeating himself. The world, an echo.

Leo snatches his Baretta off the floor and this simple motion sends already uneasy shadows scampering off, leaving him alone inside this room, which remains a living snapshot straight out of the hotel's past.

Somehow, it's fresh and pleasant and oddly preserved, though Leo doesn't question how. Just knows it was plucked from space and time—the hotel eager to prove it had once been more than a demilitarized zone.

In here, Bing Crosby sings and Leo closes his eyes, settling on his own long-dormant memory. His mother humming "Just One More Chance" from the kitchen while slicing carrots and celery on the cutting board.

How far does this illusion stretch? Can he take the elevator back to the lobby, walk out onto the street and ride the train back to Pennsylvania 1931? Visit his childhood home and say hello to his long-gone parents over a hearty bowl of chicken soup?

No. Pleasant memories are for men who wake up each day and believe the best is behind them. Fondness for the way the world once was. That's all nostalgia is. Ignorance masked as innocence.

Leo no longer has that luxury. In his world, he's come to understand the mess has always been here. He's just prone to it. His entire stinking generation has done nothing and now it's too late. The world's on fire. A lifetime of ashes in his mouth.

A young woman stands posed in the bathroom doorway, hair soaked, thin strands framing her pale face. A sheer camiknicker dangles off her shoulders. She regards Leo for a moment, eyes shimmering with playful curiosity, then steps into the room proper.

"You ain't blown yer wig yet," she says, words thoroughly animated as she bends over the dresser, studying herself in the mirror, plucking a few overgrown eyebrow hairs, turning her head to examine her cheek, completely casual, as if used to the presence of odd men inside her room.

"Am I supposed to?"

"Makes no difference." She touches a blemish on the edge of her chin and *tsks* at its discovery. Then she goes to the bed and sits down. The springs heave beneath her weight. The palms of her hands go flat on the sheets as her head tilts all the way back. "Got my own problems, ya know?" She says this with an elongated sigh.

Leo sits in the chair and studies her. Her throat stretches when she swallows and her lips pucker to draw what can only be described as restless breath. Something troubles her and, unlike those half-formed bodies that moved around in strange blurs, she really is here with him.

"Are you . . .?"

He cannot finish that sentence. It's asking a question he already knows the answer to and does not wish to have confirmed. Ignorance has a way of making things easier to process and endure.

But this cageyness irritates the young woman who's suddenly looking back with equally scrutinizing eyes, wondering why he's wasting her time.

"It's going to be alright," Leo tells her dryly. He knows so little about comfort and connection that this assurance lands with an admitted thud. He's always springing into action after the helpless are beyond help, long after they've been ground into dust by cruelty and hatred. Leo himself is as warm as a cry for help.

"Don't, okay?" she tells him. "It's just a show at this point." She forces a smile that's anything but funny and tilts toward the window. What little bit of warmth was present in her eyes has vanished. Inevitability getting her back on track.

The mattress bounces as she lifts off it, sauntering back to the dresser where she shoves a hand inside the pocketbook there. "Got fifteen cents to my name," she says with a nasally laugh. "Yours if you want it." She removes a tube of lipstick and twists it out. Studies the cherry red tip with moribund eyes and then presses it to the mirror, coloring the glass red, not stopping until it's all filled in.

"Wait," Leo says.

She ignores this, cocks a head to admire her work, then throws the tube to the floor. "Beats a hospital bed," she says, resigned.

She slides open the window and the city that's supposed to be there simply isn't. The world beyond the Steinmann is jet-black oblivion. The hotel, a tower planted in the middle of non-existence.

Outside, the howling wind is a million malevolent whispers rushing to escape the void.

The woman steps onto the ledge, undeterred by anything. Her camiknicker flaps, forming around her curves. She glances at Leo one more time, face ablaze with sudden madness because that's what you need in order to do what she's doing.

"Abyssinia, darling," she says.

Then jumps.

Leo shoots up out of the chair and then freezes, instinctively waiting to hear the impact of her descent. The sound never comes and what's left is a deafening wind delivering last rites. He pulls the glass back down to the windowsill and rests his forehead against it, wondering what it is he's still doing here.

Silhouettes return to crisscross the room at his back. Each figure projects cautious body language that suggests their continued apprehension. Leo clocks these vacant figures as reflections in the glass, all of them standing posed, turned toward him as if demanding an answer for what has just transpired.

Leo shakes his head. "Everybody dies," he tells them as if that absolves him of all responsibility.

The room's door swings open in response, bouncing off the wall. Beyond it, the wind whips so hard snow is falling sideways inside the hallway of the Steinmann.

An unappealing path. A stark contrast to the coziness of this room, which feels now like a weigh station on the road to extinction. He won't stay here. There's work to do. The skittish figures clear a path forward as he moves toward the corridor, their bodies swallowed whole by the shadows, disappearing in an instant.

Just before he's clear, a hand lurches out of the pitch-dark bathroom, startling Leo as it curls around the jamb.

Shadows peel off rosé cheeks and a familiar face rematerializes. The young lady who's just gone out the window. She's dressed in a sequined jacket and her silky hair is up in a bonnet. The cherry red lipstick frown is misery personified.

She looks older like this and gives Leo a knowing grin suggesting she remembers their encounter. This chills him more than anything. Being on the radar of spirits.

"Next show's in fifteen minutes," she tells him with tears streaking down her face. And then she closes the door and the shower's running.

3

THE LOBBY IS ONLY SLIGHTLY busier when Leo returns to it.

A twentysomething woman in high heels and a bathing suit bottom wedged into the crack of her ass slams her fist down on the golden countertop.

"Louie always gives me an hourly rate."

Behind her stands a teenager in sleeveless denim, an Iron Maiden patch embroidered across the back. His eyes are plastered to the round of her butt and he's got a wad of cash in his fist as he dances from one foot to the other because his big plans could be derailed at any second by Mister Compassion working the desk.

"I don't know Louie," the clerk tells her with complete unflappability. "But it's twelve dollars."

"Jesus!" the woman says. "You want this kid to drop his Skittles in an alleyway?"

"Why would anyone stay here?" That question comes from an elderly woman hunched on an old sofa in the sitting area, jade cigarette holder pursed between her lips. She laughs as she asks this while her gnarled and bony finger traces the cushion's cigarette burns. Holding court for an audience of none. "This is my first time here, if you want to know the truth," she says. "And it's lovely. Just lovely. Divine."

"Five," the hooker's saying. She's got her hand in the desk clerk's face, fingers stretched outward to emphasize that number. "More than generous for this shithole. And we'll be, what? Fifteen minutes?"

"Oh, I'm paying for an hour," the kid says.

"Very cocky," the hooker laughs.

The old woman scrunches her face and slots an unfiltered cigarette into the end of her holder. "People complain about everything, if you want to know the truth. They've forgotten how to be content."

Her eyes rove the lobby without ever landing on anything. It isn't clear she can even see.

"What floor are you on, ma'am?" Leo asks.

"I've never had a cleaner room. Or met a nicer staff. They even bring delicious food to my door every night. A feast. What more could a person want?"

The hooker and her teenage john pass them on their way to the elevator. "You just bought a ticket to the best show in town, honey," she says.

Leo catches the clerk glaring. His discolored skin is downright sickly from here. The way his head is angled down while his eyes are swiveled up makes him even more sinister, illustrating his disdain.

Leo waves as he walks to the exit, standing at the top of those four stairs. It's nighttime in the city now and the awning above the sidewalk is lit up so the constant shuffle of people outside continues to manifest as silhouettes.

Not unlike those in the room on twenty-one, spirits begging for help. So too does the city need him.

I can leave, Leo thinks, but he's not so sure. Blood Thunder will claim more lives. Children whose obituaries he'll skim in the paper, then crumple the newsprint in his fists because he could've stopped it all right here.

He turns back toward the lobby and the clerk is still glaring. Except now he's got a phone receiver in his fist.

Sure, Leo can leave. But he isn't going to. He's going to meet whoever's waiting for him on the twenty-fourth floor.

A YEAR ON
TWENTY-FOUR

1

RAKE IS IN 2401 AND the silver Panasonic boombox blares in his lap. Patti Smith's "Piss Factory" rattles the walls. He thinks she sings pretty good for a cunt. He's got angrier tapes, every act he ever caught at Mudd Club before that joint became a scene for hangers on, but Patti knows how it is.

Most of his tapes don't cut through the bullshit the way she does. Run the rat race? Why? For what? For scraps? Rest of the fuckers on these tapes are too busy singing about nuclear annihilation, police brutality, government wars. It's like complaining the sky's blue.

Rake doesn't care about any of that. He doesn't feel it. Shit's bad, but only in the abstract. You want hell? Go stroll the Lower East Side. People twisted up into fetal curls on sidewalk corners, desperate souls selling broken merchandise for quarters, small kids laughing as they bounce on bloodstained mattresses, and check the sunken faces of those shambling off to earn a wage that's only good for surviving another day in fuckin' zombie world.

The city's dead. These five boroughs are its graveyards.

The phone rings and Rake dials Patti down to nothing because nobody ever calls up here.

"What?"

"Hey, hey," Turbo says down at the front desk. Rake likes it when Turbo's working 'cause he's more obedient than a junkyard dog. A little powder in his bowl and he stands guard all night. "Someone checked in."

"First time for everything, asshole."

"The Man checked in."

"No chance." Rake feels around in the dark for yesterday's *Times*. "Paper thinks The Package is down in Mexico on another bender."

"Hey, just passing it along." Turbo disappears with a click.

It reminds Rake it's been a minute. He reaches for the partially scorched Holy Bible on his dresser. No idea how it got burned but he likes the ominous feeling of those charred pages whenever he flips through.

A sign he's become too powerful. Like, even that asshole in the sky is looking down with impotent fire.

When Rake first came into the Steinmann from off the street, laying low from a city that hunted him, the Good Book with its burnt pages was the first thing he found, sitting on a bed table beneath a scrawl of runny graffiti that said, THEY MUST BE PUT TO DEATH.

Rake picked it up and turned it over in his hands, thinking, *Something to pass the time.*

His fingers became black with char as he read and he'd brush that ash on his forehead in mockery, his own little black mass, while outside the summer thinned and became the frosted fall. Rain lashing the windowpane. A precursor to an even colder winter, where shells of ice entombed the windows, converting sunlight into pockets of frost.

Wasn't much, but the hotel became home. Fifty bucks every two weeks and nobody in the Steinmann would even know he was here because nobody ever comes all the way up. He got a routine going. Hide out. Walk the halls. Meet the locals.

Rake recruited a couple junkies off the street while he plotted his way back into the game, but it was this Burnt Book that got him thinking about a change of plans. Otherwise, he might've made the same mistakes all over again.

Old Testament God taught him how to think bigger. Fire and brimstone, better than those horror movies he pays to see on 42nd Street. The Good Book is the best kept secret when you want a fix of the fucked-up shit.

He re-reads its burnt words often, cheap thrills becoming inspiration. God wrecking his own kingdom, poisoning the ocean, raining down one hundred-pound hailstones in between devastating earthquakes.

That is how you rule.

At one point, the bastard gets so pissed he regrets creating humankind, decides they gotta be purged with a devastating flood. The Lord don't dig the way Egypt has enslaved the Israelites so he's gonna stick 'em with ten plagues that turn the Nile to blood, afflict man with all sorts of sores and boils, then send an angel down to hack apart the firstborn son of every Egyptian household.

Sword and sandal splatter movie shit.

Think bigger, asshole.

Precisely what Rake's doing.

He places the book down and picks up the claw hammer beside it, then goes into the hall, swiping it back and forth as he walks, keeping his reflexes honed. He loves the sound of those whooshes, though they're even more satisfying when they're followed by the heavy thunk of flesh and bone.

He used to smash whores with this thing. See if he couldn't break their jaws in a single swing. Only he kicked that habit in favor of bigger things and has no time to remember those small time days. In truth, those thoughts inspire shame because he despises his common beginnings, no better than any other thug.

Think bigger.

The Package is stashed inside 2420. Right near the stairwell. An intentional location, because the last three landings are lined with anti-personnel mines and a couple of claymores on the roof. Anyone tries to breach and this place gets blown to Kingdom Come. The Package as collateral damage.

Whoops.

Rake hopes that ain't gonna happen, though, 'cause he's got something better in mind.

"Wake up," he says on entrance, flicking on the light and catching a groan from Georgie who can barely lift his head off the bathroom floor. The open sores on his face are streaming pus and he barely seems human anymore, let alone a politician's son. "Time to take your medicine."

Rake slides the product from his pocket and tosses the packet down.

"C-can y-you do it?" Georgie barely manages to get the question out. Can't even get up onto his forearms. Just rolls onto his side and lies there wheezing.

"No. I'm tired of doing it."

Georgie tries to say something else but it's a hopeless rasp. His body ignites in shivers while beads of sweat drip from the ends of his frayed hair.

"I want you dead," Rake tells him. "I'm waiting for you to die."

"I'll die," Georgie says, eyes becoming more animated now that he thinks he's found a way to get what he wants. "I swear, I'll die. Help me one more time, please. One more time. Then I'll die if that's what you want."

Rake gets to his knees where the smell of piss is more fragrant. This junkie lives in the toilet but he can't be bothered to use it. Not only is he taking forever to die, he's fucking up the place.

Rake pops the bag and pours a few lines in front of the asshole's face.

Georgie sniffs the first before the second is all the way down, a contented vibration in his throat. It's like pouring a can of slop into the dog bowl and watching the family mastiff gobble it up as though it might otherwise disappear.

Rake turns the light off on his way out and disgust follows him back down the hall.

2

THE ELEVATOR IS OPEN WHEN Rake rounds the corner. The inside of the cab stares back. Rake stops, tightening his fist on the hammer.

If someone's up here, they must be hiding in 2401 because it's the only open door. Normally Nirvana and Stomper are here to keep an ear out, but they haven't been back in almost two days and he knows what that means . . .

It means he's a one man show again.

He hurries forward, moving along the wall with the hammer raised overhead because you've got to be vigilant in this line of work. Can't relax in your own fuckin' home because someone's always got a score to settle.

2401's empty. The bathroom sink sits flush with stacks of hundreds. He hasn't been robbed.

"So where you'd go?" he wonders beneath his breath, mildly disappointed he's been denied a reason to use his hammer.

Three rooms on this floor have been converted into a processing area and divided into chambers. He checks those next. In the first is the product he buys, the stash now entirely depleted. Next to it is his laboratory, where he cuts the snow with epinephrine, then repackages it and places it into holding—the third and final room where he's got bricks and bricks of Blood Thunder. A name he does not care for, though Rake does recognize the benefit of branding.

Nobody's out there naming that Jamaican garbage he got sent to Sing Sing for peddling.

It all goes away tomorrow morning. Couriers are coming to take and distribute this Blood Thunder far and wide. The stacks of money on his sink are to guarantee their loyalty to see this through. Blood Thunder will be so far up this city's ass it's going to be years before they can get every last ounce off the street.

Rake finishes his sweep of the rooms and confirms he's alone. Just him and his handcrafted plague, about to be unleashed from on high.

"God told me to."

There's irony in this outcome. His last base of operations, The McCauley Mission on West 32nd, shared a building with a porn shop and had one of those JESUS SAVES signs directly beside a neon pink XXX. It invited too much attention. Hard to be discrete when people kept wandering in looking to praise Jesus for saving porn from the evangelicals.

Rake was just a dealer then. Small-time thinker. Today, he's learned to be much more than that.

He's got the Steinmann to thank. Their unspoken agreement is mutually beneficial, his black heart powering the hotel like a battery. There is no shortage of bad people in this city, though most bad people are simply desperate. And most good people are only one or two unlucky breaks away from becoming bad.

Evil is different. Or indifferent.

That's Rake, who got his name after a couple months of living here, telling his boys how his job was to clean up the streets by dragging people into the gutter. "Rake 'em along, the way my father would drag leaves out of his yard, letting them wilt and disintegrate in the tree line."

His parents are still alive and living in Hoboken, as far as he knows. He hasn't spoken to them since he was sixteen and feels no connection to them or anyone. They never beat or abused him, and his childhood was generally pleasant, though he was always aware it was little more than a façade.

Every time the family took a trip into the city, the sights and sounds confirmed something inside him. And later, when he was old enough to sneak out on his own, start moshing around with other losers inside East Village dives, there was only one conclusion to reach: The city is just too sick to survive.

Like God in the Old Testament, Rake knows he's doing the Big Apple a Big Favor. And that's where Georgie comes in. Because when it's happening to the blacks and the Ricans, and, poor whites too, the city gets to shake its head and speak solemnly about the tragedy. Make empty promises and then squeeze communities already on the brink—like they're responsible.

Rake's shit is cut to kill. A ride so wild it stops your heart. Only way to expose those upper class 'recreational' users. He works hard to ensure his stuff swims upstream. Manhattan. On the jitney to the fuckin' Hamptons. Whether that works or it doesn't, he's got Georgie snow blowing his way through a couple grams because Georgie's his insurance policy. The death that's gonna tie it all together. Make it so the city can no longer deny what's happening.

Complete New York's transformation into The Poisoned Apple.

Politicians are real good at pretending it's just junkies killing themselves. Once the mayor's son is crucified inside the lobby of the *Times*, "decent" people are gonna realize they've been had. Safety as an illusion. They'll look to their leaders for answers and protection and their leaders will show their asses because they're nothing more than a department store rack of empty suits. And Rake will have conjured a genuine panic because people can't quit addiction and every hit off the street is a game of Russian Roulette.

"You better die," Rake says spitefully beneath his breath, thinking of Georgie and his one-track junkie mind.

He dials Turbo again. "Elevator's scrap, man, sending up air."

"I'll make a note for maintenance."

"Sure they'll get right on it. Order up a pizza, okay?"

"Hey, man, like I was saying, that guy . . ."

"Okay, okay. Fuck. What's he asking for?"

"He don't know his ass from his elbow."

"Then order up a pizza. 'Roni and bacon."

"Just leave this guy be?"

"Follow him if you're so fuckin' concerned. Shank him if he's a problem. You know I'll take care of you."

"Was hoping you'd say that."

"I got the movers coming at dawn. Make sure they know the route through this place."

"I'll be here all night."

Rake hangs up, figuring there's got to be a connection between whoever this guy is that's got Turbo so spooked and his missing lieutenants. Coincidences are like ghosts and neither one exists.

Although Rake has heard stories. The scariest thing he's seen in the Steinmann had fuck all to do with spirits, though. Was the day some junkie dragged her four-year-old up here and tried to sell her off for a gram. Ten lines up the nose.

Once you realize humanity's got no bottom, how are you supposed to be scared of rattling chains and creaking floorboards? The Steinmann has never felt any obligation to reveal those elements to him. It is content to absorb Rake's energy into its walls, go bleeding down, nourishing the hotel's very foundation.

Rake just thinks he's developed a stellar business acumen. What he doesn't realize is the hotel has grown so dependent on his energy that it protects him, planting rogue intuitions in his head that he's grown to mistake for natural ability. He feels trouble coming in his bones because the Steinmann is telling him there's trouble coming.

It's coming now. And there's too much on the line to leave it all in Turbo's hands.

He reaches for the dented metal case tucked beneath his bed and takes the Colt Python Revolver out, feeding six hollow points into the cylinder.

He doesn't know Leo yet, but the hotel does. Leo is twenty stories down, looking to come up. Rake senses him. What he doesn't feel, and what he's oblivious to, is the conflict stewing inside the hotel. Belief that Leo might make an even better long-term tenant.

Rake studies himself in the bathroom mirror. Dark circles beneath his eyes look like grease paint, a kind of jungle camouflage. His bleached hair is somewhere between surfer blond and silver age. His sleeveless tee reads NAPALM and he's got a striped tie fastened against his bare neck in perpetual "fuck you" to the 9-to-5 assholes who go willingly to slavery.

Pigs at a trough, swallowing all the shit their overlords serve, thinking they're getting a piece of the action instead of measly scraps.

Real change is impossible, but he's going to stop the world from turning long enough to strip the emperor of all his clothes. After that, chaos. A preferable way to live.

Some people are born evil and some buildings are built bad.

Rake never wants to be anywhere else.

And the Steinmann loves to hear that.

3

FOR THE FIRST TIME ON twenty-four, the lights are flickering.

Rake moves into the hall to investigate, gun barrel pressed against his cheek because he believes in carrying himself with confidence, especially when threatened. The lights click out and the elevator closes before his eyes have a chance to adjust.

That's when the car inside the shaft begins to descend.

And yet, he senses another presence. A stranger he cannot see. He points his gun at the gloom because there's a fine line between self-assurance and recklessness and nobody gets the drop on him inside his own castle.

At the end of the hall, something detaches itself from the shadows. Erratic motion. A body propelling toward him. High knees, lanky arms going out then up, out then up. Rhythmic action tuned to music that isn't playing.

The person isn't walking. But dancing.

A hand-jiving shadow, close enough for Rake to pluck some details out of the penumbra. A man in a suit, waltzing, each motion carrying him along with the kind of forward stride belonging to a professional.

Rake presses against the wall, retreating out of the way, gun dipping in confusion as the tall and lanky stranger continues its hop, passing him by, turning its head to regard him, allowing Rake to glimpse him in full, despite the gloom.

The dancer has no face. Just the shape of one. What's there is closer to a walnut shell, rippling folds atop broad shoulders. There's no suit on his body, only the skin of his neck dangling in a way that suggests collar flaps. The impression of an outfit when it's just layers of discolored flesh.

The figure waltzes past and its wrinkled head continues to twist, locked onto Rake, taunting him. Before Rake can shoot, the figure lapses into the darker crush in front of the elevator door, vanishing as quickly as it appeared.

Rake is left with a thundering heart, fear in his bones telling him it was an omen of what's to come. The feeling subsides pretty quickly and there is no lasting introspection or capitulation. This vision—if that's what it was—reaffirms what he already knows: He'll be dead before thirty. Possibly by breakfast.

All that matters now is getting the chemical apocalypse under way. Push it out. Achieve immortality.

Write a song about me, you punk rock fucks.

Maybe Patti will.

The Dancing Man reinforces something else. The idea that death might happen prematurely. As in now. Before the end can get under-way. The man downstairs, whose presence began as an itch, is on the verge of becoming a full-blown rash. Holding out till dawn is not guaranteed and the Steinmann has nudged Rake along because the hotel is curious to see how badly he wants to succeed.

Only Rake is determined to die in infamy and the hotel knows Leo has come to make that a reality. Rake was born bad just as the hotel was built that way, though Leo is different. He'd been human once, possessed of love and empathy. For the Steinmann, a corrupted soul is the sweetest kind. A delicacy.

"You want me?" Rake says, unsure of who he's even speaking to. He's agitated because life is never easy. Even at the end it's gotta be a pain in the cunt.

The Wrath of God is in motion. Apostles coming to take away the thunder. If he has to smite one more human being in order to buy some time, that's easy.

Might even be fun, though he'll never admit that. Gods are sup-posed to be beyond human urges.

"Not urges," he tells himself, straightening his posture, "punish-ment." Rake's gotta come down off his cloud and slaughter the vigilante. He's a firstborn.

Maybe then this shitty place will give him a peek behind the curtain.

THE DIXIE LOUNGE

1

ANGELA DOESN'T LAND WITH A thud. She lands with a splash.

The shock of a cold shower. Water where it shouldn't be. The bottom of the elevator shaft is a swimming pool. Angela isn't falling anymore. Only sinking.

A light source gives the water an incandescent quality that reveals detritus floating all around. Utensils, cloth napkins, a cracked vase. Angela orients her body and squints toward the source of the glow, paddling toward it. The water ripples and wobbly echoes tickle the bones in her ears.

She kicks through the gloom and holds her breath. Her cheeks are chipmunk puffs, small bubbles slipping past her lips to create patterns in the glowing water. The odd and seemingly impossible light source forces her to regard the way forward through narrow slits in her eyes where the bottom of the shaft resolves, suggesting a way out.

She swims hard, paddling into the aqua gauze funnel where blue-fish schools dance around floating baby strollers and opened parasols.

The path spills into a wide-open room. Circular tables are arranged several feet below, spread along a ritzy, checker-patterned floor. Golden candelabras adorn the walls alongside paintings somehow undamaged.

Angela paddles down and drifts along the bottom. She weaves

around chairs somehow anchored into place. They're immobile even when she gracelessly bumps them while attempting to navigate a path out.

Her lungs burn with impatience. The pain inspires panic. She cannot drown. Please, no, not after all this. Her heart pounds and each beat pulses through the water like radar. She envisions the hotel itself being alerted to her location, as if that fear makes any sense. But fear is irrational, and she cannot help that hers has swollen.

She paddles out past the last of the dining tables. The water stings her eyes and now she's forcing them to stay wide because she just needs a way out. Her arms have drifted out to her sides and maybe it's the lack of oxygen getting to her brain, but they're now stretched like taffy in this moment, drifting through the water like bundles of seaweed.

In this distraction, she collides with a thick slab of bar that catches her upside the head. Her world goes white, a hail of bubbles in her face, and then her skull is throbbing and a thin string of blood pierces the water as she kicks to climb above the obstruction.

Now she's overlooking a row of stools lined all the way down the bar and perched atop each one is a skeleton in old-timey clothes, all of them wearing shredded rags, streamers dancing along their bones. They're all sitting at attention, swaying in the gentle current powered by Angela's kicks, forging the illusion of dead things being somehow excited by her presence.

Angela fights to keep her mouth from opening. She no longer has the luxury of fear. *Find a way out*, she tells herself, trying to forget about her rapidly depreciating lungs.

Beyond the bar is a floor sign, black letters arrayed with a silver border. "Welcome to the Dixie Lounge," it reads. "Brand new in '32." The sign does not appear to be greeting anyone. The wall space beyond it is oddly blank. Two white stone gargoyles are balanced atop Roman pillars on either side of discolored wall space. A spot where grand doors might've stood but have since been walled off.

The light shifts as she glides into the center of the room where an abstract structure is bathed in bright streams of alternating red and green, shifting strobes from an otherworldly source. Ceramic benches line the perimeter of the formless sculpture. At one time, this had been a place to sit and drink while waiting for a table, and the interior is filled with impossibly dry desert sand and jutting cacti.

A silver traffic door ebbs in Angela's current on the far side of the decor. The kitchen entrance. She pushes toward it over the top of the ceramic installation. Her listless and perpetually outstretched Gumbi hands are useless, scraping along the tops of all those cactus spines, slicing her palms, turning the water into crimson clouds.

Her cardigan is suddenly ensnared, anchoring her. She can't swim any further, can't use her hands to pull it clear.

A desperate groan manifests as a cluster of bubbles. Her head's getting heavy but Angela continues to kick, feeling the fabric of her sweater tearing against the cactus' persistent hold. One more push and the cloth cleaves off her body.

She glances over her shoulder and it's fluttering on the plant's arm, this old watery tomb claiming an anachronistic souvenir.

Angela paddles onward, pushing open the traffic door and realizing her arms are back in scale with the rest of her body. She swims into the kitchen proper, expecting it to become her tomb. The skeletons in here are tuned to her entrance, corpses in chef hats and tattered aprons haunting long dormant responsibilities.

The corridors of ovens and freezers and stoves inspire a sense of rapidly expanding hopelessness. Too much ground to cover for what little breath she's got left. The mounds of her cheeks are threatening to deflate. If that happens, the Dixie Lounge claims more than just a sweater.

Except there's a way out . . .

Just past all the bony debris is a latch in the wall. A dumbwaiter. A stroke of dumb luck. Her ticket to another floor. She pushes the latch open and slips headfirst into the confined space that's darker and colder.

Kicking off the dumbwaiter's floor, she launches up and breaks the surface, finding fresh air, gasping to keep it. Lungs softening at last as her puckered mouth continues grabbing all she can get.

Her palms press against the sides of the shaft, flexing them to create the required tension needed to lift herself up and out. Only her hands are slick from water and blood and now traction is impossible.

Angela pushes her back against one side of the dumbwaiter and presses her feet against the other, knees higher than the rest of her body. She does this to inch up out of the water, spider-walking, pinning her shoulders and pressing her feet, forcing enough tautness between the two to be able to ascend. Her body squeaks along, constantly broadcasting her escape.

The surrounding darkness is unnavigable, as unending as a

midnight and starless sky. From somewhere below is a loud splash. A body trudging through waist-high water. The unexpected noise, the presence of someone else inside the shaft, makes her stop, but the only sound inside the dumbwaiter then is her shallow breath.

Whatever's beneath her isn't the problem because a piece of the chute above the rounds of her sneakers suddenly bursts open and light spills through in the second before a slab of glinting silver launches toward her face, halting an inch away from her eyeball.

It hovers there and Angela presses her head against the shaft, unable to get her face any further away. If she moves half an inch forward, her eye slices open like a grape.

She holds the panic in her throat, cannot afford to tip the assassin to her exact location. The blade remains stationary, a predator attempting to catch the scent of its suddenly elusive prey. It winds back, scraping through the punctured hole as it retracts its path. And then it's gone, only a thin slat left behind to ignite the shaft.

The exit is a few feet overhead. She sees it clearly now and is on the ascent again, scrambling.

The knife comes tearing through once more as though the wall is tinfoil. The blade catches her foot, wedging inside the rubber sole of her shoe. The would-be killer's hand wobbles, tightening its grip on the knife handle, attempting to pry it from the rubber.

"No, no, no," she cries and continues to slide up toward the bottom of the hatch that's nearly within reach.

The blade slashes through the wall again, striking from an impossible position, the attacker coming at her from between floors. She cries out in shock as the steel kisses the side of her mouth, tearing a divot between her lips. A dribble moves down her chin as the weapon draws back for another stab.

Angela continues her climb, every newfound hole in the shaft lighting her way forward, allowing her to plot each motion. Her fingers close on the bottom of the latch and she's pushing up, moving it into the open position, flooding the dumbwaiter with sodium light.

Her hands close around the ledge and her body goes vertical so she's hanging there, about to climb.

The blade anticipates this and stabs through the shaft somewhere beneath her torso. She feels a snake bite in her thigh that cuts to the bone. The knife embedding itself in her femur.

"Oh God!" she cries as one of her hands slips off the ledge, reaching down on instinct to try and tend the pain. The knife winds back, about to spring forward again. Angela realizes this and quickly returns her hand to the ridge, using what little strength she's got to lift herself up and climb through.

She crawls out onto an old silver food cart and pushes aside the domed tray to stabilize herself, taking a moment to catch her breath. Then she rolls off, feet touching solid floor. Blood spreads down her leg, plastering her pants to her thigh.

"Jesus, what now?" The door glides open and someone's there, tapping the wall to find the lights.

With a click, Angela shrieks at the sight of a young man in a brown leather coat, a mane of fur across its shoulders.

He's every bit as startled: Angela, dripping with blood from at least three different injuries, looking like that crazy bitch from the movie where her classmates drop a bucket of pig's blood on her.

"What the hell?" he says.

She rushes toward him with a limp, but he doesn't want her blood all over the coat he just bought and hot steps into the hallway, hands up by his chest to halt her. He's had a day, and the hotel doesn't pay enough for this.

Only Angela is too far gone to mind any such gesture and wraps her arms around him anyway.

"Please," she cries. "Please help me to get out of here."

"Gah, dammit!" His coat's covered in bloody fingerprints now, but he retracts this hostility as he clocks the damage to her body and reads the desperation stenciled across her twitching face. "Where'd you come from?"

"I don't know," she says, suddenly remembering the knife in the shaft, shrieking at the thought of her attacker following her up through the opening. "Please, take me out of here now. Right now!"

"Okay," he says with bedside manner. "Just got off work and I'm about to leave. This way, alright?" Between the guy with the gun on twenty-one, and now this, he can't wait to get out. Just a simple walk down one flight of stairs. He can bring her that far and then it's the lobby's problem. "I'm Ruben."

"Ruben," Angela says, happy to lean on him for fear he'll otherwise vanish just as Gerald and the entire third floor had.

He extends a hand across her shoulder to help stabilize her, trying to forget about the blood smears on his new coat, telling himself he can always send management the dry-cleaning bill.

They'll laugh and sign me up for mandatory overtime.

GRAFFITI TOMBS

Angela glances over her shoulder and a mini squeal slips out of her bloody mouth because she's expecting her attacker to be there. To continue his pursuit. But the hall is so vacant and silent it's to the point of mocking.

She's soaked through to the bone and everything in here smells like wet dog, and they pass a large room of laundry machines and linen racks. Then an employee breakroom. Storage areas stuffed with cots and blankets.

"What do you do here, Ruben?" It's the only thing she can think to ask. Anything to fill the silence.

The young man doesn't answer. He shakes his head. Stops moving as they're about to take a corner. He cranes around instead and mumbles something beneath his breath in Spanish before adding, "This ain't right."

It's a dead end, only the hotel forgot to hide the EXIT sign, which presides over a naked patch of wall space. Or perhaps it didn't forget at all. Perhaps it wants them to know they're spending the night.

"Nah, man," Ruben says, "ain't right at all." His hands rove the smooth, unfinished surface that ten minutes ago had been the elevator, and his brain feels busted.

Angela's starting to cry because she's seen this before, down in the Dixie Lounge, and understands what's happening.

The Steinmann isn't going to let them leave.

2

"I KNOW WHERE WE ARE." Ruben is defensive, leading them corridor to corridor with frustration.

Angela can only limp so fast, falling behind as they loop into another passageway exactly like the last. Evaporating details. Empty walls and ceilings. The hotel as a fading memory. It's all slipping away.

"Doesn't matter," Angela says, calmer now, beginning to accept the strange world they're facing. "Hey, I need you to stop. We have to—"

Ruben doesn't stop. He's a pace or two away from a jog as if he might be able to outrun the hotel's diminishing landscape.

Angela, from the opposite end of the blank corridor, attempts to explain how this has already happened to her.

He doesn't want to hear that. Doesn't want to hear anything. Keeps insisting he knows all there is to know because he works here. Knows his way around and that's his rationale for why "This can't be happening."

Some people don't do so well in bad situations. Problem is, you never know if you're going to be one of them.

"This is what it does," Angela says, applying pressure to her leg as she hobbles along. "My client on three tried to spell it out for me. He was so terrified and trying not to show it . . ."

Neither of them could know the Steinmann has never in its fifty

73

years been as powerful as in this moment. Driven by opposing forces, the man up top who thinks he can destroy the city, but also the man on their floor with the gun in his hand—currently headed toward them from a parallel corridor.

"You're crazy!" someone screams from up ahead. The heated tone makes Ruben stop, giving Angela time to catch up, leaning against his blood-smeared fur shoulder so to give her leg a break. "Stay the hell away from me!" the same voice shouts and then someone is running, hurried footsteps racing toward them.

The guy who bolts around the corner in a pink suit jacket is familiar to Ruben, his face igniting with mutual recognition before a pop sends him flying across the corridor, crashing against the wall, his back going flat against it.

"No!" He lifts a hand in front of his face as a second shot comes from the corridor beyond and two of his fingers explode. His hand squirts blood straight to the ceiling. His head lolls toward Ruben and Angela and a single red tear trickles down his cheek because one of his eyes has been blown out and his brains are dog chow on the wall he's now gliding down.

The man with salt and pepper hair who appears at the corner, lowering his pistol as he crosses himself, is also familiar to Ruben.

"Hey, man," Ruben says, immediately animated as though his life depends on appealing to the executioner's good graces. "I told you this was how to go upstairs, remember? I wanted to help you!"

Angela isn't listening. She somehow understands the old man with the smoking gun is not her problem. It's the corpse she's unable to take her eyes off.

It's been a long time since she's watched someone die.

BONEFREEK

1

"WHY CAN'T WE LEAVE?" RUBEN asks, hovering in the doorway to keep watch, one nervous foot jittering in and out of the hall.

"Just turn around," Angela says, waiting until he does to strip off her blood-soaked pants, little whimpers of pain as she rides them down her thighs while Leo takes the first aid box off the breakroom wall.

"Up on that table," he tells her.

"It's not going to let us leave," Angela says, doing as he asks. "I can't explain it."

Leo hasn't asked her to. He douses a cotton ball with hydrogen peroxide and daubs the stab wound on her thigh. Every touch an electric shock and she squeezes Leo's forearm to brace against the pain.

"You murdered someone," Ruben says. "Right in front of us."

"Told you I wasn't a cop." Leo continues his work on Angela's leg, no interest in justifying himself further.

He's too calm about this, Angela thinks. The way he wasted a guy like taking out the trash. It can't be the first time he's done it.

Leo unspools a roll of gauze around her thigh and clips it into place, then attempts a smile that's colder than the wind. "You'll live."

"Promise?"

"I never make them."

A promise is what Angela is after, though there is an odd comfort in Leo's craggy features. A hardness that comes with age, wrinkles on wrinkles slightly offset by his squinty blue eyes—small pools reflecting the slightest trace of humanity. That's fine with her, given this mess. Only way to fight evil is with more evil, which makes them best friends tonight.

"Well," Angela says, "thank you."

"Thank you?" Ruben says, watching Leo from the door where his shock has manifested as indignance. "For what? Executing a coworker?"

"He didn't want me taking the elevator."

This pisses Ruben off because a man like this could easily get the wrong idea about him and his pals as they're walking home from the movies one night. A sideways glance from any one of them being all it might take to provoke his suspicion. His action. A man like this . . . *Nah*. His style doesn't sit with Ruben.

Though the feeling is mutual in Leo's mind and he returns the pointed stare, wondering if every Steinmann employee serves the man upstairs. "You ever do things outside your job description?"

"Psh." Ruben waves a dismissive hand. "My whole job is outside the description."

"Like what?"

"Ad said '*Other duties as assigned*' so you can't complain when they tell you to take a hose into the bathroom 'cause somehow there's shit on the ceiling."

"Oh, gross," Angela says.

The kid shrugs in response because he's seen worse. "Bellhop's still gotta work when there ain't enough guests to tend to. Look, man . . . I'm the one who told you about the elevator and you're looking at me like I'm guilty. I don't have time for this. Gotta get home. Now."

"Yeah," Leo says, "you mentioned your father." It seems to him this kid is on the up-and-up. He's got a light in his eyes the city hasn't extinguished. Yet. A soulfulness that cannot be faked because nobody here has time for performances, not even the Steinmann itself, which seems to regard its role as a place of lodging only on occasion.

"What about your dad?" Angela asks. "What's going on with him?"

But Leo's continued eye toward Ruben makes the bellhop

nervous and that's the conversation he clings to. "I barely knew the guy you shot," he says with added defensiveness. "Don't think I ever said more than '*hey*' to him."

Leo swabs both of Angela's hands and then bandages them before going to work on the slice at the corner of her mouth, gentle daubs at first to test the sensitivity of the wound and then clearing the blood away when it's obvious she can take the pain.

"I've read about you in the paper?" Angela says, less of a question and more of a gentle accusation.

"And you've got all sorts of opinions."

"Lots of people are scared of you where I work."

"Where do you work?"

"I'm a social worker so the whole city's sorta my office."

"Noble."

Angela can't decide if that's sincere or mocking and chooses the latter because she's learned to be defensive. "More noble than shooting people."

Leo presses the gauze square against her mouth with a little more force than Angela thinks is necessary. It stings for a moment but then the pain is gone.

Definitely mocking, she decides.

"Almost done," Leo says, applying medical tape to the edges of the patch on her cheek to keep it in place and all he can think is, *What a nuisance*. He's babysitting children. The social worker is slightly older than the bellhop, but he can't be bringing either of them up to twenty-four. It'll be like pushing a stroller through a warzone.

Only he can't abandon them in the bowels of this hellhole, either.

"I'm just grateful for the company." Angela hops off the table and hobbles across the room, wincing with each step. The pain remains, but now that she's been patched, it isn't as debilitating.

She chooses a pair of men's slacks off the floor beside the employee lockers and has to make a new hole in the belt to properly cinch them, keep them from sliding off her thighs.

A stack of baby blue Steinmann Hotel shirts are scattered across the far table. She slides one over her shoulders and it falls past her hips. She glimpses herself in the mirror and finds she resembles people at the shelter whose wardrobes are mismatched and based entirely on charity—whatever they can cobble together from the kindness of others. It makes her realize she's got a chance so long as she's alive.

"You two should stay here," Leo says. A half-hearted suggestion without anyone's well-being in mind. He's unable to look either of them in the eye as he makes it. "Lock the door when I leave and—"

"You're joking." Angela limps over and gets nose to nose with the vigilante. "You think that little of us?"

"Had to try." Leo starts toward Ruben who's still in the doorway, only Angela isn't done arguing, grabbing his elbow and forcing him to spin back around.

"I just went for a swim in the hotel's flooded ballroom."

"What ballroom?" Ruben asks. "There's no ballroom."

"Well, there you go," she adds. "I'm pretty sure I did, but my brain is filled with a fog I've never felt. Don't know if that's my rationale trying to protect what's left of my sanity or if I've already lost that."

"You haven't," Leo says, the kind of thing someone offers as a precursor to more comfort, though in his case, it's the only two words he's got.

Somehow, it's enough for Angela and she releases him. "We're your partners now, Mr. Vigilante, whether you like it or not."

"No way," Ruben says, the idea of following this stone killer around the hotel after dark is sickening. He steps aside to allow Leo to pass into the hall.

"We're staying together." Angela brings her fingers to her collarbone. "I'm Angela and you're . . . Ruben, right?"

He closes his eyes and knocks his head back, unable to believe where this night has gone. Where it could still go. "Yeah," he says.

"And you're . . ." Angela adds as she and Ruben follow Leo into the corridor like lost puppies, where the old man is studying part of the wall that had been more than a vacant patch of sheet rock on the way in.

"Leo," he says begrudgingly.

The Steinmann's geography has returned, but only in partial. There are no windows to climb out of, and the elevator is still just a blank wall. Only the stairwell is accessible, and as they pass through the door, they realize there is no way to reach the lobby. The descending stairs are simply not there.

Ruben shouts something in Spanish, stomping the flat floor as though this is an illusion that can be shattered through force. "I have to get home!"

"It wants us to go up," Angela says.

"No way." Ruben shakes his head.

"Come on, broken record." Angela tugs him along by his bloody coat flap because nobody is getting left behind on her watch.

They're following Leo as he climbs toward the next floor. He doesn't know what's happening any more than Angela or Ruben, and their mutual confusion helps to clarify the Steinmann's powers in their minds. This fellowship has exorcised their individual fears of insanity. No choice but to accept these sights and sounds as a new truth. Each has felt the transmogrification in their bones, a hotwiring that allows the acceptance of this world as a place of impossible possibilities.

And if you can cast aside the dread this place inspires, there's inspiration to be found because now you're among the chosen few. Leo feels this awakening, though it is buoyed by an even worse nagging in his gut. A question that's been gnawing at him ever since he stepped out of his room on floor sixteen.

How do I kill what's already dead?

The gun in his hand might as well be a feather. He used it to blast down two thugs this morning and another just now, but the further he climbs, the more weightless it becomes.

On the first landing, Leo stops and waits for Angela to catch up. "How do you know that?"

"Um, what?"

"That it wants us to go up."

"Because it's letting us." Her tone suggests this is obvious, though she doesn't fully believe that to be the case. The hotel did everything in its power to prevent her from escaping the Dixie Lounge, and the more she reflects on that, the more empowered she becomes. The Steinmann is not infallible.

Leo may not inspire warmth, though there is something immovable about him which makes it easier for Angela to continue climbing. The idea that he will not allow them to lose without a fight. It isn't much, but it is a chance.

"So we're going exactly where it wants us?" Ruben yanks the fire axe off the landing wall and holds it tight, adjusting his stance to the weight it brings. "All I had to do was keep walking when I heard you screaming . . ."

"Oh come off it," Angela says as they resume their climb. "Think of it as a story you get to tell your kids one day . . . right before they commit you to Bellevue."

"That ain't cheering me up."

"I'm trying."

"Try harder," Ruben says with desperation. "Please."

"Okay, well, how long have you worked here?"

"A year."

"Come on."

"What? You think it's like this every day? What's happening here is every story I ever heard. Whispers and legends and shit people say to one another on smoke breaks. It's all coming true in one night."

They're nearly to the third-floor landing, putting Angela right back where she started. She watches the door more tightly wound than a rabid dog, envisioning it swinging open, that knife-wielding killer leaping out, blade in hand, using its other one to yank her back inside. She pictures Leo and Ruben's indifferent faces staring in from beyond the glass, unwilling to risk their own extinctions to prevent hers.

Leo just loops around and starts ascending toward four and Angela is so close to him that she's pressing against his back. Happy to continue climbing out of hell.

2

RAKE GOES DOWN TO TWELVE where Sassoon, a junkie whore who took her street name off an advert for finishing rinse, is shivering atop the bedsheet.

He clicks the room light on and she stirs, then stretches, her hands folding around the headboard so her body bends upward with a gentle groan. The light catches a spurt of crusted semen on her thigh and abdomen.

"Fuck," he says, "you look gross."

She *tsks* and yawns, squinting against the jaundiced bloom of light that's spreading, grimacing once it becomes clear he isn't turning it back off. "I wasn't expecting company," she says.

Sassoon has track marks on her forearms. Tiny patches of black and blue. Rake sits beside her and lifts one elbow to take a closer look at his merchandise. Her scars are puckered mouths, each hole somehow opening and closing, slurping noises sucking air, desperate for something—*anything*—to latch onto.

The hotel continues taunting him. First with the Dancing Man and now this. Unexplained occurrences are suddenly commonplace—visions intended to spark something inside of him. Some deeper knowledge of the Earth as a place where the barriers between the living and the dead are down and have always been, where the netherworld is always there, free to walk up and reach out—

"No," Rake says, dropping her elbow onto the mattress, then rising to stand flat against the wall. Not far enough away from the disgusting contagion on her arms, though the distance is going to have to do.

"Hey," Sassoon says. "I never hid my habits from you."

"Yeah, but . . ." He isn't sure how to say it because she's oblivious to the animated track marks, dragging her fingers along her arms without regard for the mouths trying to catch them in the same way a newborn tries latching a nipple. It's like she doesn't see them at all, and how can that be?

Rake isn't going to raise the topic because it'll just get in the way and complicate his reason for coming.

"I'm careful," she says.

"We're past worrying about careful."

"I'm not." This comes out in a growl. "Just 'cause I work for you don't mean I don't like my life."

He cannot stop staring at her forearms. Junkie holes as fish mouths, begging for needles, each of them promising a faster route to her bloodstream. Zero to nuked in less than five seconds—and all they're asking for is a little prick.

Why doesn't she notice?

Rake's eyes aren't bugging—the holes *are* there—and his mind ain't the problem. Things have gone south since the Dancing Man, that skin hanging off its body like a ballroom tux.

Act like a god, asshole. It's what he's trying to do but the Burnt Book suggests visions are insular, meant to reveal certain spiritual truths about the one witnessing them. That's what disturbs Rake. What is he supposed to glean from these?

"Shit," Rake mumbles. "I'm overthinking everything." He's unwilling to raise the issue here. Leadership inspires less confidence when your lieutenants think your brain is a cracked egg sizzling on a sidewalk.

"Overthinking?" Sassoon asks.

"Can you put some fuckin' clothes on?" Rake says. "I wanna put you to work."

"I just went to bed," Sassoon moans.

"I don't give a shit." He's tempted to backhand her across her eyes but doesn't want to touch her gross-ass skin.

Sassoon groans and rolls over, giving him the royal view of her heart-shaped ass. Her best asset and what her regulars pay top dollar to fuck. Truth is she's getting too high on her own supply, but it doesn't matter when she's got a body like a Rolls Royce, top of the line and fun to drive.

"Let me sleep awhile," she says softly.

"That's all you do."

"'Cause I *work*." She lifts her head and glances over her shoulder so Rake knows he's touched a nerve. "I earn you money . . . which is waiting for you on the dresser, by the way. So take it and let me rest."

"Nah," Rake tells her. "That's yours." He isn't going to squabble over a cut when there's an assassin coming to kill him.

Sassoon is still craned around, looking past Rake, clocking the doorway he left wide open. Her eyes ignite, gasping at the flickering yellow glow spilling in from the hall. She scrambles off the bed and slams the door, throwing her back against it like she's trying to keep something out.

Rake is so surprised by this urgency he laughs, and his spite provokes her ferocity. She attacks with a two-handed shove, palms against his shoulders. It knocks him off-balance, sends him staggering.

"You stupid b—"

"You know the rules!" she growls over him.

Rules? He's never paid her superstitions any mind and sort of regrets that now. She sells her holes and the only time he gets involved is when a john becomes a problem. If he's gotta bash in a skull or pluck an eye from a socket with the claw end of his hammer, so be it. Then it's back to her. That freedom is what makes their partnership so appealing.

"I've told you what's out there," she says off his silence.

"Tell me again."

"Whatever, Rake."

"For real . . . I'm interested. Tell me."

"I just know . . ." It's a pause because Sassoon still thinks he's busting on her, but Rake's focus is concrete. Concern that raises her concern. "It, um, travels these halls at night. In the dark." She reaches up over the door and taps the crucifix nailed to the wall. A string of rosary beads is tacked around the frame and she gives those a good rub too, beginning to mouth a quiet prayer.

"You're talking to God, a god that lets you live like this," Rake said to her once, arguing how God in the Burnt Book is as cruel and as merciless as the meanest mother he's ever encountered.

Yet she believes.

"God has a standard," Sassoon had replied in argument. "If he thinks we strayed, we can't be surprised when he decides to smite our asses. Instead, we need to be grateful he noticed us at all."

Rake snaps his fingers, breaking Sassoon's Sunday morning concentration. "Once you're done with mass, I got a job for you."

Sassoon tilts her head to one side, ear-to-shoulder. "You mean you really don't believe in it?" She steps away from the door as if "it" is enough of a mention to summon the thing she's scared of.

"In what?"

She puffs her cheeks, beatboxing as she creeps toward him with fingers curled into claws, lips flapping, laying down a Grandmaster Flash beat while channeling her best Melle Mel. "*Bonefreek got a mean streak, body like an antique, find him and it's bleak, ah huh huh huh huh . . .*"

"I don't want to hear that shit," Rake tells her. "Kids on a playground."

"And I don't want that motherfucker summoned to my door."

"Come on."

"You could always let me back up on twenty-four." There's sugar in her voice now. "Plenty of room up there, you'd never even know."

"Can't have your johns coming and going. Any one of them could see something and—"

"Then respect my rules." She points to the rosary.

"Time to pay off your debt."

"Rake, what the hell? You don't want money, but you're sending me out to work?"

"This is different." He pulls open the dresser drawer and rummages through until he finds a pair of orange hot pants and tosses them on the bed. Then he's searching for a top and settles for a shear long sleeve that's probably too hot but shows off her tits while hiding her monstrous arms. "Put these on."

"Since when do you dress me?" That's when she knows this job is beyond the needs of a demanding client. The way Rake refuses to look at her ignites a trail of gooseflesh up her already itchy arms. She scratches them and Rake makes a sound like his gut has turned to curdled milk. "You're being fuckin' weird."

"You need to get close to someone. Bring that nailfile with you and—"

"No. No way. I'm a Christian."

Rake laughs so hard the walls shake.

"I'm serious, Rake . . . I don't do that."

"No one leaves this life with their hands clean."

The crucifix above the door conjures memories in Sassoon and her eyes drift to the hammer in Rake's hand, suggesting the one thing that will happen should she refuse his order, though it's maybe preferable at the end of the day because death is always better when it's the devil you know.

"*Bonefreek got a mean streak, body like an antique, find him and it's bleak, ah huh huh huh huh . . .*"

If Sassoon has to die, at least Rake will kill her with a hint of mercy. Maybe even love. That'd be nice.

"You get to keep your legs closed this time," Rake says. "Asshole too."

"Even if that's what he wants?"

Rake is silent, which means he's thinking things over and Sassoon breathes a sigh of relief—glad he's at least chewing on it. She's never even had to think about killing someone before. "You mean . . . bring him up to ten and . . ."

"Why not?" Sassoon says. "While he's going to town on me, you do what you gotta do. I don't even need to know when it's coming."

"You think you can find him?"

Her body's shaking because her soul is in open rebellion—*Do not do this*—begging to stay inside tonight. There is no choice. Rake's one employment condition is that you never tell him *no*. Tell him *no* and you'll find yourself in a bathtub, that hammer raised high, eager to smash—

"So how 'bout it?"

Instead of answering, Rake goes into the bathroom and slams the door. Looks himself over in the mirror, glass littered with the residue of a million popped pimples. Sassoon's gross-ass complexion always hidden beneath a cosmetic cake. He feels powerless tonight and understands why: the Steinmann does not consider him a god and never did. The hotel is rolling out lessons in humility. Reminding him who's boss.

"Why now?" Rake growls. "Why at the very end?"

"You know why," his reflection tells him and Rake feels a tug on his tie as if a hand has reached out of the sink and grabbed it.

He leaps back with a startled yelp and the tie is out in front of him, horizontal like a pointed finger. Whatever has it, wants it. Wants to yank it away. He hears Sassoon stirring just outside the door, probably got her ear to it.

"Hey—"

"He's old and carries a gun," Rake shouts, yanking the tie out of the spectral grip, sighing in relief when it's back to being flat against his chest. "That's all I know. Find him and bring him to ten."

"And you'll meet me there?"

"I'll meet you there."

"How am I supposed to know where he is?"

Rake's reflection cracks a smile Rake himself is not making. In the mirror, he holds up both hands as balled fists and raises fingers until eight of them are wiggling.

Sassoon is tired of waiting for him to come out. She dresses in the clothes he likes, forgetting about the crusted jizz on her belly because the anxiety in her chest is too painful to endure. The idea of going out in these halls after dark. The risk of running into that which terrifies her. It's why she works days.

"*Bonefreek got a mean streak, body like an antique, find him and it's bleak, ah huh huh huh huh . . .*"

"Eight," Rake shouts, muffled beyond the bathroom door but also sounding totally unhinged. "He won't see it coming."

"Say, uh, maybe you could escort me down there and—"

"Move your ass," he screams like a whipcrack.

And that's exactly what she does.

3

THE PROCESSION OF LEO, ANGELA, and Ruben climbs in a tight cluster, passing the eighth floor where Ruben's attention is drawn to shimmering window glass, a blunted sparkle like fresh-dug diamonds in a mine.

Leo hears the young man's footsteps trail off but isn't interested in stopping. He loops around the landing toward nine, though the sound of an opening door forces him to slow. "Ruben," Angela says from below, "what are you—?"

"How?" Ruben asks. A monosyllabic question peppered with panic. "How are we supposed to escape when it can do this?"

Leo comes back down and catches sight of the bellhop just before he disappears onto the eighth floor. Angela is by the door on the stairwell side, looking to Leo for guidance, as if he is supposed to know how to wrangle this kid.

"He needs to start accepting some things," Leo says, thinking again about how he needs to unload these two. How he doesn't trust himself to keep these glorified children safe. His world is easy because of the binary he lives by: Frontier justice and gunpowder ghosts.

Ruben stands just inside the hallway and the floor defies expectation. A wide-open space standing in contempt of the Steinmann's blueprint. The bellhop flanked on all sides by an army of converging shadows.

Leo raises his gun out of habit but there's too many of them and not enough bullets, reaffirming what he's long realized: He isn't shooting his way out of this.

"Back up, kid," Leo says. "Toward me. Do it now."

Ruben starts to turn and the closest shadow, a dark figure of matched posture directly on his right, does the same, pivoting in modest delay.

Leo aims there but spots another silhouette in the distance with a gun pointed back and the confusion in Leo's mind quickly resolves itself. This is not an army at all but a kaleidoscope of reflections. A hall of mirrors where even the floor and ceiling are reflective. Leo looks down and sees himself glancing up. He glances up, and there he is looking down.

An overwhelming sense of vertigo takes him, is combined with the notion of drifting through a spaceless void, and Leo staggers against a pane of glass, groaning as instinct overrides his thoughts.

"Don't look at anything," he says, sounding frail and tired and every moment of his sixty years because he's terrified of what's coming next and will do anything to avoid it. The sight of himself with a gun to his temple, ready to squeeze the trigger.

"What is this?" Ruben shouts as if his reflections are equipped to answer, each of them stands as wide-eyed as he is, dozens of insane faces reflected. "What the hell do you want with us?"

"It'll get worse," Angela says, using Ruben for leverage because her leg is throbbing again. "If you keep freaking out, it'll get worse . . . and then it will kill us."

"Keep moving," Leo mumbles, winded and inching toward the stairs, suddenly scared to death the hotel might decide to yank their escape hatch out of existence and leave them stranded here in madness.

Angela seizes the flap of Ruben's bloodied coat, attempting to tear him away from the spell of his own personal doppelgangers.

He's resistant to follow, transfixed by the reflections breaking formation, moving independently of Ruben, pacing and walking, some even dancing to music that cannot be heard. "You seeing this?"

"Yeah," Angela says. "I was stabbed climbing out of the basement through a dumbwaiter. A basement you told me doesn't exist." Her reminder of how much better Ruben has it at the moment.

Leo is able to open the landing door, breathing with relief while behind him, their reflections glare ad infinitum. For a moment, there's a fourth figure gliding along inside the refractions, but he blinks and then it's gone.

"I had a conversation with a girl who jumped out a window," Leo says, the most relatable he's ever been to either of them. "Just before she reappeared in the bathroom."

"We've all survived," Angela says, grunting as she pulls Ruben along because he remains captivated by all the other Rubens, especially the one doing a back spin on a cardboard foldout. "For now."

Leo continues to hold the door open, attention zeroing back onto that disassociated shadow creeping through the glass again. A single figure moving without restriction across mirrors. Its dark trench coat flapping behind its stride while the wide-brimmed fedora casts long shadows that disguise its features.

He goes cold at the sight because he's seen this killer before, earlier this morning and twelve blocks away.

"On the move!" he shouts, the shadow rising behind one of Ruben's many reflections, its hand flicking back to reveal a straight razor tucked between skeletal fingers.

Ruben flinches as Leo takes aim in his direction, certain in this moment he's about to be shot. He dives to the floor, pulling Angela with him as Leo fires a bullet that rushes over their heads, disrupting the stagnant air with a whoosh.

Only the bullet disappears into the gloom, hitting nothing, despite their world of all-encompassing glass, and the figure vanishes from sight and Leo is back to fishing inside the glass, searching the unending sea of reflections for another trace of that trench coat.

From the floor, Angela shrieks, writhing around to evade something only she can see.

Ruben is back on his feet, dragging her by an arm, though her ankle isn't budging. It's elevated and somehow locked in mid-air, anchored to nothing, held by no one.

What's got her is only visible in the ceiling, four reflections deep and it's so slight it's easy to miss. A skeletal hand closed around her ankle, weighting it in place. Leo looks at the real Angela writhing before him and there is nothing holding her there, yet Ruben cannot budge her one more inch.

"Alright," Leo says beneath his breath, pressure like he's never felt. The bone white hand sits at the end of his iron sights. He holds his breath because if he's off, he'll clip Angela's reflection, and the hotel is petty enough to take its anger out on the flesh and blood social worker whimpering at his feet.

"Help me move her!" Ruben screams into Leo's ear.

The gunshot shatters the bone into dust. Angela's leg plops to the floor and she scurries like a frightened cat, scrambling and bumbling into Ruben during their shared race for the stairwell.

They collide with Leo and all three of them go spilling across the concrete slab as the door slowly heaves closed behind them.

On his back, Leo takes aim because the sound of footsteps—clacking nails striking glass—has never been louder. And then the specter is watching from the other side of the door window, pacing with all the frustration of a junkyard dog.

They're staring at the monster, pure terror pumping through them and their spirits are breaking down, wilting in the presence of something so alien and unfamiliar. A sight they shouldn't see, let alone so casually.

It wants them to know it's hunting them.

"Shoot it, man," Ruben urges, but Leo shakes his head because it's too late for that. Bullets cannot fix this.

"Three of you?" The question is asked by somebody standing behind them. A woman in hot pants and a see-through top, whose make-up is so hastily scrawled it looks as though someone has applied it to her.

She leans on the railing, attention bouncing between them, but reserving all her smiles for Leo.

"Aren't you a fun bunch?"

"I know you," Ruben says, glancing to the window, which is empty now. The space beyond it back to being the Steinmann proper. Dirty corridors and filthy rooms. He takes a second to catch his breath and then adds, "She hooks out of Room 1012. We're not supposed to know that, but people are always asking us to point the way there."

"Sassoon," she tells them. "And it's honest work."

"Is there another way out, Sassoon?" Angela asks.

"You want to get out?" Sassoon bites her cheek to prevent a smile. She knows she's got one of those faces you can't trust, and any expression at all will mark her true intentions. That's not what she wants. What she'd like is precisely what the three of them are looking to do.

Escape.

It could happen fast. Before Rake would even know they're gone.

He'd come looking, of course, because her debt hasn't been paid. And that is the very thing he's offering. Her debt for this old man.

She's at a crossroads, wondering which path is more likely to carry her along. She's been here before, though, and always chooses poorly.

Leo sizes Sassoon up, but he's wrestling with his own notions of hopelessness. In these last ten years, he's always succeeded in destroying his prey. Tonight, every ounce of instinct he's got is urging him to turn tail and run because this isn't the kind of place that lets people go. He's seen enough to know that much.

Maybe nobody ever gets out alive.

Or maybe that's the hotel talking, grinding him down because that's the only way *it* can win.

"We need to get out of here," Angela says. "Like yesterday."

"Sure." Sassoon is chiseling her thumbnail down with her trusty file. "I'll help you get out, and all you gotta do is follow me."

4

THEY MOVE IN PAIRS UP the stairwell and Sassoon doesn't look them in the eye. She's never had the stomach for this. They seem like nice people. She's always wanted to know nice people.

But sometimes parents die when you're a kid and your life is one long tumble through the state system. All Sassoon has to do is mention this and Angela would perk up. It would get the two of them talking, Angela offering ways to help. And Sassoon would begin thinking about how if the years had aligned better and she had gotten into Angela's caseload, then maybe her entire life could've been different.

Could've been good.

But that is not going to happen because Sassoon has taught herself that *what ifs* are a down payment on a future you can't buy. Even if these three can help get her out of the Steinmann, she's better off alone. She doesn't trust people to pour her morning coffee. That's the benefit of a downtrodden education.

"Uh, you all mentioned you were trying to get out." She glances at Leo's shoes, sees he's already clocking her from the corner of his eye. "What do you mean . . . *trying?*"

"You know," Leo tells her.

"Seen some shit, huh?" Sassoon says, smaller and less boisterous than her usual showroom persona, Leo's loaded words confirming she should never have left her room after dark. After dark is when people go missing.

"What have you seen?" That question from Ruben.

To Sassoon, he's the young man in the bloodstained coat directly behind her. She thinks he's been staring at her ass because of how her cheeks peek out from the seam of her hot pants. They have their own gravitational pull when it comes to wandering eyes.

Only Ruben is too scared to be thinking about hard-ons. He suspects she's in bed with the man upstairs and worries she's about to make life more complicated. But he's so desperate to escape he's willing to chance it.

"Not much," Sassoon says, "but I'm nine to five. Being awake this time of day is new to me."

"Your pimp gives you nights off?" Ruben asks.

Leo stops mid-climb and shoots a look over his shoulder because he's reading between the lines of what Ruben's throwing down. "How do you intend to get us out of here?"

"There's a laundry chute."

"That isn't going to happen," Angela is quick to interject.

"Ain't no laundry chute," Ruben says pointedly.

"Hotel ain't used it since I got here," Sassoon tells them, heart pounding while on the precipice of choice. Maybe she does give Rake the slip tonight, but bad men are a chronic illness and will always come back to finish you off once you think you've got a clean bill of health. "We can use it to go all the way down."

Leo and Angela turn to Ruben, their expert on all things Steinmann. He shakes his head but stops because he's second-guessing himself. "Shit, it's an old building and it ain't like I studied the blueprints."

"They say it goes down to a part of the hotel that ain't in use no more," Sassoon tells them. "Old train terminal or something."

"Where?" Ruben says.

"Ten. Hidden away inside a maintenance closet."

Ruben nods because he could be convinced this is the truth. "How do you know this?"

"We drop our paraphernalia down there to get rid of it."

"Sounds real enough," Ruben says, eager to get everyone's eyes off him. Can't stomach the responsibility. Life's plenty difficult when it's just his father to worry about, let alone factoring in the lives of strangers.

"It's real," Sassoon says, overwhelmed by the possibility of getting out. How she'll go someplace far. Her brain keeps pushing West Virginia, but the pessimist in her says she'll be selling herself for meth and moonshine inside of a week.

As the saying goes, wherever you go there you are.

She gives Leo a suggestive smile and adds, "We could get them out, and then I could get *you* off."

They're nearly to ten now and Leo stops cold. His companions do the same. Sassoon doesn't get the hint until she's on the landing above them. Turns back to see Leo with his arm draped across his knee, gun in hand and she knows she's blown it. Too far, too fast.

Leo's first instinct is to shoot her dead, though he is vaguely ashamed of this. A spy can be turned. Can tell him everything he needs to know about the man upstairs. What he's walking into.

"Hey," Sassoon offers a nervous stutter. "I'm just saying, I got a safe place and I know loneliness when I see it."

Leo figures he was made the moment he came through the Steinmann's doors, but his prey is hiding behind this strung-out junkie. Cowards are cockroaches—survival at any cost. That tells him plenty.

Angela makes a harsh sound like all her breath has been sucked out of her lungs and Ruben joins her in a sudden expression of shock, mumbling something in Spanish Leo doesn't understand. They're suddenly inching back down toward the landing below, faces frozen forward.

"What the hell are you . . ." Leo's words trail off because then he sees what's got them so startled.

A swirling shadow taking shape behind Sassoon. That familiar hat rising out of the darkness. A razorblade glint like a striking match as her neck is sliced wide. The arterial blast catches Leo in the face. The sting of hot splatter in his eyes sends him staggering and he grips the railing to keep from falling.

The hooker's eyes pop with exaggeration as color abandons her complexion. The blade cuts through the soft of her underarm, gliding down until cold steel bounces off her hipbone, the newly carved vertical gash slicing the shirt off her body, unleashing Sassoon's gasping track marks, a dozen mouths popping in one synchronized gasp before blood oozes out of them like a lawn sprinkler.

From the black crush glides one bony hand to caress the vertical incision along Sassoon's body. Fingers crawl the wound where the razor has cut most deeply, skeletal appendages slipping in up to the knuckles, closing, tightening, and then tearing her flesh with the ease of shucking corn.

Sassoon's slack body collapses against the belt-coated shadow, her neck lolling to glimpse the face beneath that wide-brimmed hat. What she sees there brings her back to life, re-animated for one final full-throated scream that manifests as a wad of bubbles foaming through her neck wound—every hidden secret the world's got announcing itself through the presence of this gravely unholy thing.

Find him and it's bleak, ah huh huh huh huh . . .

The Bonefreek works its victim, tearing Sassoon's skin aside to unveil gorgeous bones beneath, hands coiling around her dripping rib cage, fingers clacking along as if playing an ancient instrument. The creature purrs with the sound of rusted metal as it snaps off part of her skeleton.

Sassoon gasps with every crack, and though her eyes are on the verge of rolling back, she manages one last look at her murderer and feels the crush of hopelessness as it spreads head to toe—somehow understanding that it isn't simply her life being taken, but her eternal soul as well.

The absence of light. Her greatest fear, realized. Her consciousness preserved in a state of permanent despair.

The Bonefreek gives an otherworldly cluck as it pulls its cinched belt loose and its coat falls away from its waist to reveal what's underneath. An inhuman structure holding no biological function. A chaotic jumble of bones. An indiscriminate fusion culled from every species, mismatched and discolored, bonded together in zigs and zags and in utter contempt for Mother Nature.

It continues snapping ribs away until Sassoon's sternum is vulnerable and within reach. One of the Bonefreek's skeletal hands is much larger than the other and that one makes a fist around the center bone before breaking it off and tearing it clear.

The hooker's body collapses in a mess of flesh and bone as the creature holds the sternum high. A moment of triumph that Leo, Angela, and Ruben are intended to witness. It presses the bone against its own makeshift body with a sizzle and the sudden smell inside the stairwell is that which accompanies a dentist's drill: Decaying cheese on a summer night. The sight of the Bonefreek adding another piece to itself is a sickening sight, the creature dragging one showy finger along its length to show itself off, admiring its unique existence.

Leo has the creature in his iron sights and fires, knowing in advance the futility of his attack. He empties the magazine and his accuracy fails to disturb the creature at all.

It makes no motion to fight Leo, gliding right past him, descending upon the two people several stairs below, Angela and Ruben shrieking like terrified children in each other's arms.

Leo ejects the spent mag and slots another, drawing this time on Ruben and Angela. His gun barrel hovering between two possible targets. "I'll kill them," he says. "Quick and easy deaths. You'll get nothing."

The wraith lets loose a frustrated clack that implies it does not doubt Leo's threat, slinking into a pocket of deep shadow and never emerging.

Just like that it's gone, dissolved into the void with only a puddle of splatter on the landing above to prove it was here at all.

Leo has never seen a person reduced to less in a matter of seconds. Pure precision as it executed on the purpose for which it was created.

Angela draws heavy breaths and uses the railing to resume her climb, limping ahead without any reaction at all, just grim purpose because this night is getting worse all the time.

"Good thinking, man," Ruben says. He taps Leo on the shoulder as he goes by, an affirmative gesture supported by genuine appreciation in the eyes. Try as you might, you just can't hate a man when he goes up against the devil on behalf of your life. Ruben makes the sign of the cross while approaching Sassoon's remains, knowing this encounter will haunt him until the day he dies.

Leo crosses himself as well and then gives Sassoon a wide berth as he steps onto the tenth-floor landing.

5

NOBODY HAS ANYTHING TO SAY. All three of them with the backs of their hands beneath their noses because Sassoon's remains are smelling worse with every second.

Above them, the path to eleven is blocked by a metal gate. Behind it, a dump of broken bed frames, headboards, old toilets, and torn mattresses. Even if they could pry it open, there's too much junk to clear away. The route is impassable.

"What happened to the guests?" Ruben asks, shaking his head because this hotel continues to mess with him. This blockade wasn't here earlier, just like the mirrors on eight. He worked a nine-hour shift up and down these floors today. "There's people staying here, man. Where are they?"

"Maybe they're asking what happened to us," Angela suggests.

"Was she telling the truth about the laundry shaft?" Ruben asks.

"Was hoping you'd know," Leo says. The Steinmann hasn't persuaded him to alter his course, but if he can get these kids out, it's one less thing to worry about. Then he can get on with hunting the coward above.

"Hey," Angela says, turning to Leo. "Could you have done it?" She takes him by the forearm so he can't break away. "Could you have shot us?"

"Let's go," Leo says, the answer somehow present inside those two simple words.

"You saved our lives . . . by threatening to kill us." A harsh laugh because this is what passes for humanitarianism inside the Steinmann. "I guess I just want you to know that if it comes to that again—"

"Yeah." Leo gently pulls his arm away from Angela's hands and goes to the door.

"And yet," she continues, "maybe when we get out of here, you'll let me take you to coffee."

"What?"

"Let me make a case for why you should hang up your guns."

"Maybe we have this conversation later," Ruben says, peeking over Leo's shoulder as the vigilante opens the door and looks in on ten, the bellhop breathing a sigh of relief when the space beyond reveals a standard hotel room floor.

"No, I think we're having it right now," Angela says. "Fear and anger is what puts us in danger."

"You sound like Yoda," Ruben scoffs.

"Kid's right," Leo adds.

"People are basically good," Angela tells him.

"Tell that to the man who murdered my wife and son. You going to take him to coffee too? Talk some sense into him?"

This hits Angela like a fist to the stomach. Foot in mouth any other time. Tonight, a *faux pas* is a luxury they don't have. "I can't imagine that loss," she says, "and I'm sorry. Truly. I look into your eyes and I see the pain. What it's done to you."

"Save your sympathies."

"I know," she says. "That loss might be the only thing keeping us alive tonight. Not every story is the same, Leo. I have clients who've turned it around. Men and women who, if you had encountered them on the worst nights of their lives, would've been shot dead. Today, one's the most beloved priest in his parish while another manages a food kitchen in Brooklyn. Two people who grew from their mistakes, channeled their pain into something positive."

"Like I said—"

"Save my sympathies, right?" Angela digs her brass knuckles out of her pocket, holds them in Leo's face. "There is a time to fight. I know that better than you think. But if it's all you do, it's all you are."

"Someone has to," Leo says, eyes suddenly alive with purpose. "Half the cops in this city are on strike—"

"I'm not judging you. I meant what I said. I am grateful for what you were prepared to do back there. But conflict is what the hotel wants."

"Well, why don't you try hugging that thing in the hat next time it comes for us?"

"All I'm saying . . . Just think about turning things around when this is all over. Toward the light."

Angela knows she got the old man between the eyes, something clicking behind his long-faded blues. She's prepared to keep the pressure on when a sweet aroma fills the stairwell. A disturbing scent that sweeps away the putrid stench of Sassoon's body, confirming one terrible truth: The Steinmann is rummaging through her thoughts.

Where it has found the unmistakable scent of Hav-A-Tampas.

Cheap convenience store cigars. The only brand her father smoked. "Better than Cubans," he'd proclaim. A declaration that certainly had more to do with cost over quality. Seventy-nine cents a box.

"Tell me you smell that?" she says.

"Cigarellos," Ruben says. "People hollow 'em out and fill 'em with grass. Maybe they'll set off a fire alarm."

"We won't be that lucky," Leo says.

Swirling cigar memories tune Angela's brain back to her hometown. In Florida. It pains her to admit Dad had been right about the city, confident Angela would one day come to agree with him. That's something she cannot shake.

"People there will step over a homeless man in the gutter on their way to a charity dinner," he'd say. "Cities are for rootless cosmopolitan assholes. People who hate themselves so much they're desperate to fill their lives with meaning. For them, that's culture. It's the only thing they got."

An uncharitable assessment, Angela knew, even then, but it continues to strike a silent chord because she is always taking in theater, movies, and concerts on her days off, wondering if these preferences are simply to spite the man she despises.

Culture is a nice thing to have, she'd like to tell him. *It brings the world together.*

Ruben snaps his fingers in front of Angela's face and she's back to reality. "Hey, so long as we stay together, we're good." He speaks with the same performative sincerity she feeds her clients, which is why she knows better than to take it seriously.

The only way out is through. It's hackneyed advice, but it's also the truth. Doesn't mean everyone is going to make it.

Angela touches Ruben's face in appreciation, also for an exchange of energy. A reminder of human connectivity. Two souls struggling to remain intact in a hopeless place.

Leo steps onto ten and the skittish lights inside click off, creating a corridor where the umbra is adrift with oily swirls rotating in slow circles, conjuring the illusion of native creatures born from the dark.

"We should break for the elevator," Ruben says.

"I wouldn't do that," Angela tells him. "Unless you want to take a swim."

"Find the laundry chute," Leo says, taking aim at the animated shadows as he approaches.

The door slams so fast behind him it's practically a slap on his ass.

Angela calls out, panic over their separation, but Leo keeps walking, wall lights clicking on around him as the tenth floor wakes up, alerted to the presence of trespassers, delighted Leo has come so willingly.

Angela pulls the door open to give chase and Ruben follows. Only Leo is gone and they're on a darkened version of ten that's still awash in blackness save for the occasional flicker of busted wall lights.

Just enough for Angela to spot a fire alarm up ahead, as if the hotel hadn't thought to hide it yet. She hurries to it and pulls the plastic T, waiting expectantly for a siren to assail every floor in this tower. There's only silence. The alarm doesn't work.

"No," Angela says, hopes dashed. Only so many times this can happen before you break wide open.

"Leo," Ruben whispers, as if the hotel simply might not hear him. "Don't go too far, man. We can't see you."

"Why won't it work?" Angela cries, panic reducing her question to an impotent wobble.

"Leo," Ruben says again, fresh out of ideas and suddenly terrified of being separated from the guy with the gun.

The situation is worse now. Shadows appear and just as quickly disappear in strobe, figures poised to strike, but never do.

Not yet.

Ruben and Angela are alone and her whimpering, the sound of someone trying to keep it together and failing, spreads hopelessness through him because she's been the strong one and now she's breaking. Now they're on their own.

Leo is gone.

GUESTS

1

HILDE SITS IN ROOM 1204, knees against her chest, cowering in the corner because the man outside keeps jiggling the knob and laughing.

The phone is off the hook beside her. Every call to the front desk goes unanswered and there isn't even a dial tone now. She cups the receiver anyway because it's the only weapon she's got if the man outside happens to get in.

All Hilde wants is to go home to Germany.

She's on holiday from university because she feared this would be her one and only chance to visit the states. Everyone wants to see The Big Apple just to say they've been, and there's no hotel closer to Times Square at this price.

Now she understands why.

The laughing started on her very first night. An eruption some-time around 2:45 a.m. She sat up in bed, clutching her chest because at first she'd been certain it was coming from inside her room. Only it stopped as quickly as it started and Hilde rolled over and went back to sleep, chalking it up to an isolated incident. Some drunken passerby stumbling back to his room, perhaps.

It returned on the second night. The same volume and intensity. So precise, it had to be a recording. Somebody pulling one over on her. Hilde threw the sheet off her body and crawled to the edge of the bed, studying the slat of light beneath the door, which shifted because somebody was pacing back and forth in front of it.

She stared in disbelief as the laughter droned without pause and those silent footsteps continued to pace. She watched for so long she became convinced it was a trick of the light. The motion was just too constant and unending and nobody would stick to such a confined routine. Except the laughter refused to stop and nobody picked up at the front desk and she had no choice but to lie awake and listen to the insanity until daylight burned the corners of her window shade.

This morning she tried to complain, but the man downstairs did not speak German, nor was he interested in interpreting her broken English that she spat haphazardly from over the pages of her translation guide. She set off to explore both the Guggenheim and the Met, her trepidation temporarily staved by the wonders of this American metropolis.

It wasn't until she returned to the Steinmann that she began to feel terror in the pit of her stomach. The laughter resumed the moment she closed her door as though it had been waiting for exactly that, booming up just over her shoulder.

Hilde ran shrieking for her bed, hopping onto it, all notions of rationale vanishing in an instant, landing on the one conclusion she would've done anything to avoid: Something, not someone, was tormenting her.

The shifting light beneath the door freezes now and the booming laughter is somehow louder than ever. The doorknob spins. Hilde shrieks, remembering how her parents had pleaded with her not to come alone, but university students are altruistic and adventurous, never considering the caution of previous generations.

Whatever's outside knocks and Hilde's body jerks from the unexpected shock. She screams for help and someone from a distant room shouts back, "Shut up, cunt!" which she doesn't need translated.

Visions assail her. She flashes on two men on some rooftop, binding a young woman's hands and legs in sailor knots only to lift her at the feet and shoulders and heave her off the ledge.

A flash and Hilde sees a junkie mother pressing a bath towel to her infant's mouth, anything to make him be quiet. She doesn't realize she's suffocating him in the process.

Flash. She's watching a prostitute's last trick of the night, a deranged man with needle marks up and down his arms, who swears he's got a clean bill of health but whose joy comes from spreading the disease killing him.

The hotel's past feeds itself into Hilde, revealing the things it's laughing about. More misery than she can stand. The dismal history of the Steinmann unfolds in her mind like an evening at the cinema, more depravity than she ever hoped to know. Weaponized misery drawing her to reach a specific conclusion.

Time to check out.

Except she's hanging on and it's longer than the hotel wants. And every time Hilde thinks about running, she flashes on imagery of strange men waiting in the hall, rope binds in their fists so she understands there's only one way out of here.

Doesn't matter that she has everything to live for back home. A full scholarship and that cute boy, Jonas, who asked her to see a movie at the Metropol as soon as she gets back next week.

This conclusion incenses the Steinmann. The wall over Hilde stretches out, a face taking form in the elasticity, bending so the bulbous eyes are angled down, regarding Hilde with menace.

She springs up and something cold snaps around her ankle, yanking her off balance, the floor smashing her in the face.

She's crying into cigarette-burned carpet as her calves are split open. Then she's gliding along the rug and nothing makes sense. As she angles herself around, she sees two yellow eyes, sickly and mismatched, hotel wallpaper pulled down in front of this protruding face like a flowery mask.

And then there's the wide mouth distending all the way to the floor that's about to swallow her whole . . .

2

"I THINK SOMEONE'S IN HERE," Cassandra says. This realization prompted by their suitcase lying wide open on the floor, contents flung around the room.

"We locked the door, didn't we?" Tony asks, frozen and oblivious as to how to respond to such an obvious violation. They're from North Dakota. What do they know about being burglarized?

"This city," Cassandra sighs. "What'd they take?" She kneels and begins to rifle through the chaos, creating hers and his piles to account for what's missing. Except she doesn't get very far because what's missing is evident. Her undergarments are gone.

Tony becomes possessed with indignancy and shouts his outrage so everyone on the floor knows there's a problem. The kind of display that only matters when the place you're staying at cares about its reputation. The Steinmann has no reputation to uphold and even less of one to lose. He intends to complain anyway and orders Cassandra to stay behind as he marches into the hall.

Because of his entitled stride, he doesn't notice the door across from theirs opening as soon as he's past it. Had he turned, he would've seen the wraith-like figure glide across the hall, disappearing straight into their room, where Cassandra's on her knees, grabbing at the fabric debris.

Tony would've almost certainly noticed the glinting razor blade tucked inside its shadowy fist. And if Tony hadn't been determined to march downstairs and give this dive a piece of his mind, rehearsing a speech beneath his breath, then he would've heard everything happening to Cassandra . . .

Skeletal fingers closing on a tuft of hair, yanking her head back. Cassandra's eyes swinging up, seeing the contours of a skeletal face tucked beneath a wide-brimmed felt hat. She feels the cold sting of the blade as it lands on her throat and the immediate warmth of its kiss as it cuts her open.

Blood empties down her length, color draining off her face as her body is repainted in dark crimson.

She drops to her side, neck glug-glugging across the carpet. Cassandra's vision fades as her eyes widen. Her last thought while staring at a pile of Tony's tight white underwear is: *We should've gone to Vegas.*

Tony isn't yet at the elevators when his wife dies. He taps the button and gnashes his teeth, trying to bottle his anger. People who work in places like this are used to unhappy customers. He's going to have to pour it on in order to get his point across. In order to put the fear of God into them.

"What are you going to do about it?" Tony says in practice but doesn't like the way his voice sounds when he ends on a question. "What are you going to do about it, asshole?" He tries and realizes how much more effective it is.

He's going to have this whole vacation comped by the time he's through with this hotel.

The doors open with a ding and he moves into the elevator car as the lights inside cut out. He's standing in pitch darkness as it begins to descend, and suddenly there's someone else in here. Indicated by the tortured breathing both rusty and desperate. Something clinging to life. Or attempting to mimic it.

Either is impossible. The car had been empty.

Before Tony can question things, the wraith plugs a butcher knife into his heart, cold steel breaking through bones and eviscerating the beating organ. Tony's dead before he knows it, his body staggering around, painting the walls with streams of spurting gore.

His feet slip on the streaks and his body goes down and the blood shoots up and pelts the ceiling and just keeps spurting.

3

THE BIKINI-BOTTOMED PROSTITUTE, WHO goes by Krystal, takes the teenager's money in her fist and counts it out. Eighty dollars for three minutes of work and a jizz-glazed face. Beats temping.

The boy was embarrassed he finished so soon, couldn't wait to get away. Krystal stretches out on the bed. The cold air is refreshing on her sweat-glossed body.

She's got a small jar in her bag, a patch of foil on the opening that's taut with an elastic band. Just like a drum. A few holes poked into the foil on one round, and a small mouth cut out of the other one. She flicks her cigarette ash over the holes to create a "bed" and then sprinkles a mound of crack on top of that ash, pressing her lips to the larger hole and flicking her BIC to light the rock.

A couple of deep breaths, then it's letting the air out very slowly through her nose. She knows she should get back out there and earn, but it's cold and this is a nice escape. Euphoria, far more preferable. She chases feelings of possibility and invincibility and knows she can quit anytime she wants. And will. Soon.

Just because the high disguises these things doesn't mean the pain is gone. It's all still there, the beatings and assaults, degradation and abuse at the hands of crooked cops—nobody looks at her with more disdain than they do while also coveting what she's got.

Krystal's eyelids flutter and finds figures standing around her bed. They make no motion to touch her and simply watch. Leeches to blood, except it's her pain they're feeding on as she twists on the mattress, freely giving it away.

Take it all, please.

They're impervious to the chemicals she puts in her body. They only feel the truth. And the truth is that Krystal's pain is strong enough to kill most people.

One silhouette sits down beside her. She's vaguely aware of the inhuman, tri-pronged hand sending gentle strokes through her hair. Yellow eyes regard her fondly as they glance down the length of her body. Real awe. How is it possible for someone in so much pain to carry on day after day?

She opens her eyes and sees a dark outline in her face. She barely cares. Neither does it. She lets her eyes roll back in her head, and the silhouettes dare to come a little closer, devouring her pain along with her face.

4

BARB WAKES UP BECAUSE THE itch has come back.

"Damn," she says and reaches under the bedsheet, clawing at her calf, slow to start, then much harder, chasing relief that never comes.

Her fingernails only make things worse, but she can't stop itching, faster—her face twisted into a lemon sour squint. An elastic groan as she fights. And then the itch moves up to her shin and she's chasing it, digging in to stop it from spreading.

Her other leg itches now and she brings both knees to her face to scratch them and there's a warm wet dribble on her fingertips. She pulls her hand back to check and gasps when she sees blood.

With a tear, the sheet comes off the bed to reveal a wiggling mass of bugs scurrying in every direction. Barb screams and her legs drop back down, and it's only when they're stretched to the foot of the bed that she realizes her flesh has been scratched clean away, right down to the bone.

Bugs swarm across her legs and up her length.

With another scream, eight-legged pincers hurdle over her lower lip and vanish down her throat, sapping her breath. Her head falls back on the pillow and through wide eyes the ceiling is suddenly crawling with bugs, all of them dropping down at once, covering her, suffocating her, blotting out the world.

5

DAVID'S BEEN WATCHING TELEVISION FOR so long
he's no longer wondering how it's even possible when the TV in this
room did not work at check-in. He paid for three days board, though
he's been here a month, maybe longer. His fingernails are overgrown
when they were trimmed to the quick the morning he arrived. He's
dehydrated and shouldn't even be conscious, though he simply cannot tear himself away from the flickering image, his own personal
broadcast: Every death inside the Steinmann since inception, beginning with a hardhat who strangled a co-worker over the suspicion of
a stolen lunch pail and then dropped the body into the base of wet
concrete in order to hide it.

6

ROBERT LIES ON THE FLOOR, face peeled off two days ago, a halo of flies swarming, gradually sticking to the runny muscle mass that is his cheeks, and he's gasping and groaning, and wondering— *Why can't I die?*

BROKEN MIRRORS,
BROKEN MINDS

1

THE TENTH-FLOOR HALLWAY IS no longer a place inside the Steinmann Hotel.

Leo doesn't notice Angela and Ruben have vanished because he's moving down a sidewalk of drifting steam. The Baretta's in his hand and he's passing beneath a blinking circular sign that's got Chinese characters on it with the English name stenciled around the edges. CHI MER RESTAURANT.

Something about this seems vaguely familiar and Leo finds just enough memory to know to slip into the alley between two buildings where steam blankets everything, gushing up through cracks in the pavement.

A tuft of long hair is spilled out from behind a scatter of empty cardboard boxes. Some punk in a military jacket, a necklace of rifle shells threaded around a chain on his neck. Permanently unblinking eyes because of the bullet hole in his throat. Etched across his face is the kind of naïve shock that always happens at the end because, in a blink, the game's over and nobody ever sees it coming.

Leo does not remember this face. Ten years have unfolded in a hundred alleyways, always ending with faces exactly like this. "I don't know you," he says, though his words are troubled whispers because he understands that he's supposed to.

Details of this night are lost to time, overwritten by the dozens of deaths that would follow, though the longer he stands over this van-quished enemy, the more he remembers. The uncertainty of it all was special.

Something about this kid's face makes Leo feel ten years younger and fifty is a lot lighter and less achy than sixty. On this night, he strolled the sidewalk with two rolls of quarters stuffed inside a black sock in his pocket. A bag of groceries tucked into the fold of his arm to send a clear message.

Come take it.

The punk in the military jacket did come to take it. Leo remembers the violent shove from behind. The bitter taste in his mouth as he bit his tongue hard enough to draw blood. The way his groceries spilled across the sidewalk, one last matchstick striking flint, igniting in him the fire still burning today. The second tectonic shift to occur in Leo's life in less than one year's time. First, his family exterminated in a random act of violence. Now comes Leo's reciprocation . . .

How could he ever forget the way his hand trembled when he pulled the sock from his pocket, winding it into a weapon with his spinning wrist.

Or how the punk's eyes widened, almost comically, as it dawned on him he was in over his head, having done exactly what his mark had wanted. The quarters cracked him in the teeth and he spat two of them out.

Leo drew his gun. The kid knew what was coming and bolted into the alley beside the Chi Mer, swallowed by that thick blanket of bil-lowing city steam, banking that no one would be crazy enough to follow.

Only Leo was insane, squeezing off two shots. The first caught the kid in the back, the impact causing him to spin and face his at-tacker with his hand outstretched in a deescalating, "Whoa, whoa, whoa . . . hey, man . . ." and beginning to sputter out an apology when Leo's second shot caught him in the throat.

He didn't stick around. Now Leo's remembering how he spent the rest of that night: Telling himself he hadn't done what he clearly had—killed a boy no older than one of his students. He recalls vom-iting off a subway platform on his way home and then again into his toilet once he got there. How his hands shook for the rest of the night, no matter how much scotch he swallowed.

The first time he'd ever taken a life.

It's second nature now.

He didn't even cross himself back then.

"You want to know the truth," Kimberly says, her figure materializing amidst the steam as though she were made from it. Leo stares at the dead kid's face because it's easier than the shame of looking Kimberly in the eye. "You're always wondering if the man who killed me remembers . . ."

The body at Leo's feet never gave him a drop of catharsis. Not now and barely then. The Steinmann knows how to hurt him, though.

" . . . don't you already have your answer?"

Leo would like to argue how this was different. *"This was for you."* Only, was it? Kimberly's dead. This poor bastard had jack all to do with that. Leo had gone hunting that night because he wanted to kill. *For the good of the city,* he remembers telling himself. The only way to combat the parasitic feelings of helplessness and grief sucking his soul and draining his penchant for life.

The hotel believes the truth to be darker than that.

Leo looks at the gun in his hand and feels the recurring urge that's always gnawing at him. The one that had first assailed him earlier today on the sixteenth floor inside of a reflection. *Put that to your head and end it.*

Why? he thinks.

You have to ask? How about for disgracing the memories of your wife and son? There was a way to carry on, Leo, but not like this. You allowed yourself to become a monster because it was always inside you. It's inside everyone.

These beliefs are as alien as the urge to shoot himself in the head.

And then he's back in the hotel and running down blandly familiar corridors stamped in cold blue light that is sourced from nothing, is somehow overlayed on top of everything. Wherever he goes, the world is cobalt. The path is always angling to the right, looping around, ad infinitum, because his own squandered possibilities are what he's fleeing, and are not so easily escaped.

Up ahead is the mouth of a hotel room without a door. From Leo's vantage, there is a wall of cold metal drawers inside and he recognizes it as the city morgue on the night the fire started.

The worst moment of his life.

He mouths the word "no" and those metal morgue doors slam open in outburst. Leo leaps back, heart pumping with agitation he's never felt. His chest hurts and his face is numb and his brain screams, *I'm not going out like this.* Coronaries are for clogged arteries and old age. Not jump scares.

A ripple of static announces itself with a crackle of faltering electricity. Reality bends on a shockwave passing through space to reveal the true interior beneath Leo's hallucination. Not the morgue, just another shitty hotel room. Roaches trapped inside the light bowl on the ceiling, hairy legs clanking the glass bulb, insects knocking, trying to get out.

"I'm going upstairs," Leo announces. "You can't hurt me with the life I've already lived."

"Then how about one you haven't?" a cold voice suggests.

A figure sits on the side of the bed, knees spread apart, hands curled around them. A person only in the abstract and devoid of all detail. A blank white face with pinholes for eyes, tiny reflective orbs inside of them. It has no ears though it does turn toward the sound of Leo's approach and a ripple moves across its blank visage in the only gesture of recognition it seems capable of making.

One gnarled hand rises off its knee, reaching out, fingers still curled and unable to straighten. Leo halts in place, somehow understanding he must not touch this thing, which now begins to stand. Its first steps are a graceless last call lumber, as though it has never used its legs before.

It's inching closer, swaying with inhuman bluster, and Leo flees, rushing through the front door, and what's in front of him now is a quiet suburban street. Houses up and down the way. One side is a mirror image of the other. A dog barks in the distant night, and somewhere even further is a car alarm going off.

He glances back and the faceless figure is framed inside a doorway in the center of the street. Cold blue light attempts to spill past him, but the faceless man appears to be holding it back, cobalt hues casting his rigid body in an otherworldly glow. Leo stares for a long time because he does not want that thing to follow.

It lifts one gnarled hand to the sky and holds it there in a kind of parting wave meant to assuage Leo's concern.

"So go," the detached voice suggests.

He is going. Drawn to the nearest house where every light burns warm beyond the windows. Leo steps off the street and his nose dances with allergies from the fresh cut grass beneath his boots.

He sneezes and knocks on the door.

2

ANGELA FLINGS OPEN THE MAINTENANCE closet on
ten and slides a pushcart of cleaning supplies out of the way to reach
the space beyond it. The wall is a blank patch of unpainted sheetrock,
and someone has spraypainted FEEL ME INSIDE YOU over it.

"Graffiti marks the spot," she says, stepping aside so Ruben can
do his thing, lifting the fire axe to ready a swing. "This looks good."

Ruben brings the axe down with a huff, decimating the drywall
with a few simple cleaves to find a loose confederation of wires dangling like spaghetti. Angry hums threaten them with electric stings.

"No," Ruben says. "There's no chute here. She was lying."

A child laughs from some distant corridor and the satisfied giggle
is an affirmation of power. The kind that happens when Mom or Dad
has finally lost their patience.

The hallway lights flicker again and assorted faces bleed through
the gloom, each one born in an azure glow. Distended funhouse
heads wearing irrational grins, mouthing silent instructions.

"Give me this," Angela says and takes the axe from Ruben's fist.
She limps across the way and swings the blade against a hotel room
door, splinters flying like shrapnel.

"What are you doing?"

"Finding a room with a view." The door splits down the middle
and Angela shoulders through, goes straight for the window with

Ruben following—anything to get away from those cursed faces, only they're suddenly inside his head each time he blinks, grinning wider because there's nowhere to run.

Across the alley is an office building. Sporadic lights clicked on in some of the windows like a game of Connect Four. "I'm curious," she asks, "how far do you think that is?"

"Too far to jump."

"Is there a ladder?"

"You want to climb out there?"

"Got a better idea?"

With silence serving as the answer, Ruben instead offers an imperceptible nod because nobody ever said getting away would be easy. "Okay," he sighs. "Let's go back down and grab it."

"Where?"

"Maintenance closet. On two."

"You mean where we came from? I wish I'd thought of this sooner."

Ruben assesses the space between the buildings while the faces around him drift in and out of corporeality, distracting him, stoking his nerves, jumbling his thoughts. "Uh, I think the ladder goes twenty-four feet across. Might be enough. Only problem is . . . ain't a thing over there to anchor it to."

Ain't the only problem, Angela thinks. The hallway brims with the sound of restless bodies, shambling in perpetual approach. Monsters always coming. Incentive to stay hunkered down in here, sowing doubt over her determination.

Yeah, I'm a survivor, doesn't mean I'm always going to survive . . .

For Ruben, though, it's about a dad in the Bronx with a broken back and a bellyful of pain meds that have already worn off. An accident on a job site, some scaffolding failure where the concrete wasn't given enough time to cure because the men in charge believed they could shave a few days off the job and pocket that cash. Men who were nowhere to be found when the structure toppled and killed ten hardhats, leaving dad crippled and without the bread to buy his way into rehab.

Doctors say he's "lucky to be alive," but nothing about it screams luck. Ruben hasn't had a good night's sleep in over a year because of those screams. They're always unplugging him from dreamland in the early morning whenever the medication wears off. And that's only the start. It's the indignity of the old man needing his ass wiped when he was the kind of guy who wouldn't complain about a tooth ache. And it's the way Papá needs his food to be sliced up ahead of time because he no longer has the strength to do it himself.

For Ruben's old man, life ain't what it used to be. He no longer has any control and often complains of being along for the ride, always at the mercy of others. Others like Rosalia, a widower who lives one floor below them and spends every day in their apartment, doing laundry and changing bed sheets out of the goodness of her heart because she works second shift at an assisted living facility in Manhattan and knows about patient care. She's always sneaking supplies to them that they otherwise couldn't afford.

For Ruben, his job at the Steinmann is necessary to keep a roof over their heads, but it's also to buy a bed in the rehab center Papá desperately needs, though his greatest fear is that he'll never bake enough bread to get him there. Bad enough he had to drop some cash on a winter coat because his last one got torn apart on a subway turnstile, but freezing to death on the sidewalks of the city wasn't going to help anyone.

So much of life is running to stand still and isn't this how the world forces you to do things you don't want to do?

Ruben has had offers. Pushers and stick-up men looking for extra bodies. He's resisted their invitations. Not out of any misplaced loyalty for the bullshit American Dream, but because Papá had the good sense to point those guys out a hundred times over the years. They always look the same, even when the faces change. Guys in sweated-through t-shirts with switchblade bulges in their pockets, standing on street corners scoping people the way scavenger birds circle the skies for prey.

"Don't ever get in with them," Papá would say. "They'll squeeze every drop of goodness from your soul and you won't be able to breathe, and then your story's written and it's the kind of ending nobody likes."

The argument, as Ruben got older and started to see what honesty bought you, is that it isn't this life you have to worry about . . . but the next one. Standing on some fucking cloud, having to look your relatives in the eye and justify the things you did as if it was the only choice.

"There's always a choice," Papá would say. "When you can't see one, it just means you ain't looking hard enough."

Ruben doesn't know if he believes that, though he's resisted the urges to make a quick bit of cash to hurt somebody he doesn't know. But he's getting weak and tonight it's a race to prevent Papá from getting swept up in a tidal wave of agony. The idea he might not get home in time to stop that scares him worse than anything the hotel can throw.

"So . . ." Angela says and Ruben notes the vulnerability cresting through her face—doubt solidifying the way an egg in a skillet goes from translucent to solid white. "What do you say? Can we do this?"

She's losing the fight and it's on Ruben to show her how it's done. To carry the group for a while.

"We can," he says. "It's a good idea." This restores some of the confidence to her face so he adds, "We need to be climbing out on a lower floor anyway . . . If the hotel ever lets us find another window."

"We'll blow a hole in the wall if we need to," Angela says and the voices outside the room roar in disapproval.

That's what Ruben is talking about. Maybe Papá is right. There's always a choice. Ruben plucks his axe from Angela's hand and tightens it in his fists like he's Dave Winfield about to crack one out of right field. He marches from the room with Angela in tow, defying the doubt that's rising on waves of bile in his throat, his body screaming, *You'll never make it on time.*

Ruben is tired of screams.

The hallway is vacant despite the sound of bodies staggering around. Invisible footsteps shuffling on filthy carpet. They reach the stairwell without incident and he gives the heavy door a tug and moves through, stopping cold on the other side.

Angela isn't expecting this and bumps into his back. Their attentions are divided, hers going to the screeching in her ear, nails on a chalkboard, while on the landing below, Ruben watches a cluster of mannequins, bald heads and anonymous faces, squatting over the spot where Sassoon's remains lie. They're gobbling her skin out of molded plastic palms while their impossible teeth grind her bones to dust.

Their heads angle up in one rehearsed motion, listless expressions shifting into something illustrating their displeasure.

"No," Ruben says, stepping down to step up. Fear for his dad is driving him. Sedatives wearing off, pain revving up. Finally, here's something he can take his frustrations out on. Something he can hit.

The nightmare army regards his approach. Plastic faces smothered with blood. Their knees click as they rise, light bursting from their molded eyes and crooked mouths.

Ruben charges down, eager to start chopping but their arms spring out in unison, grabbing hold, yanking him into the center of their cluster with a surprising show of strength.

Angela hasn't noticed because a hand has looped around her arm, pulling her back onto ten. Someone she doesn't see. An all-too familiar voice squeals, "What did I tell you about this city?" before flinging her against the wall. Her head cracks off the light fixture, delivering a jagged glass kiss to the back of her scalp.

"Ruben!" she shouts, pushing off the wall and rushing to the door that will not re-open. Beyond it come Ruben's screams, frantic and terrified and severed as quickly as they start. "No," she cries. "Please!"

Then she's running down the hall, wide-eyed, tears streaking, desperate to locate a weapon or tool—anything to help pry that door open.

Why, what chance do we have? She hates the growing weakness that inspires these thoughts, then reminds herself that if it was hopeless, the Steinmann wouldn't be fighting by throwing everything at her. Including her son of a bitch father because all that's done is make her remember how far she's come.

Life had felt hopeless back then, too.

Around the corner it's a straight shot to the elevator and she's ready to risk falling again, only, before she can get there, her face slams against something in the middle of the corridor, like smashing headfirst into a brick wall. Only the brick wall is laughing and now the outline of a gun barrel looks her square in the eye.

"Thought you were someone else," a man says.

"Ruben." Angela is too breathless to consider the circumstances of his appearance. "He works here, is trapped in the stairwell . . ."

"Too bad for Ruben." The man takes the gun out of her face.

"If you could just help—"

Behind them, the elevator opens as if overriding Angela's request. Light spills out, pouring details over the man who takes her by the wrist and gently nudges her toward the glow. "Nothing you can do for Ruben."

"Please, I can't let that thing get him."

He releases her hand and backs off. Gun inching up. "What thing?"

His eagerness encourages her to become withholding. Something about his hostile behavior suggests he'll take it out on Angela should she say something he doesn't want to hear. That the person he's probably looking for was broken into pieces on the same stairwell she's trying to reach.

"Can I—?" Angela takes a few steps back and uses her head to gesture around the corner. "I mean, it's easier if I show you."

He checks his gun for affirmation and then agrees to follow, the two of them performing an awkward single file speed walk to the end of the hall where stairwell access has become another faded memory.

"How did I know?" Angela says. "It was here. Right here."

"Yeah," he says. The palm of his hand glides along the surface of more naked drywall, processing this impossible fact. That the hotel has swallowed the entryway whole. "You see anyone else?"

Angela shakes her head, which prompts him to close his eyes and offer a deep-bellied sigh in response. Something he doesn't want to do, or some plan going to pieces. He snatches her by the arm and tugs her along.

"Hey—"

"It isn't safe to be here," he growls.

The elevator is waiting when they get there, door open because the Steinmann would like them to be together. Its game seemingly requiring it.

"So we're leaving?" she asks. "Right?"

If it's comfort she's after, his bleached hair, the tie hanging around his neck, and the hand cannon in his fist, is enough to discourage it. "Not exactly," he tells her.

And the smartest thing to do, Angela knows, is be quiet and go along for the ride.

3

LEO FEELS HEAT ON HIS eyelids and a soft press of skin against his bare chest. He's back to consciousness and his nostrils are on fire with pleasing hints of sandalwood and that conditioner Kimberly used.

When she first died, Leo kept the last remaining bottle by the sink and would pop open the cap on occasion. Smell it a bit. A way to trick his brain into believing she was still there. In the other room or running errands. Not dead and buried.

Except, Kimberly is not dead and buried. Leo smells her conditioner just as he feels her hair tickling his cheek.

His eyes flutter against what he now realizes to be the morning sun pouring through to the bedroom. Suburban songs are sung in the distance: grumbling lawnmowers, that mail truck hum, the carefree laughter of neighborhood children.

His eyelids lift and gradually find focus. Familiarity in the checker-patterned bedsheets, the bureau nestled between two windows overlooking the side yard, his bottle of Old Spice always standing atop. He's had that one since 1976. It just never seems to run out. And there's that painting of the Jersey Shore on the wall because that's where they're going to retire one day.

Leo's never been inside of this room, but he somehow recognizes it.

Kimberly lies nestled against his shoulder, exhaling onto his neck so his gooseflesh is riled. These simple sensations wedge a frog into his throat.

The last decade of rain-slicked streets and bullet ridden bodies becomes a stranger's dream. Fast-fading details in the morning light, indistinguishable from all those creature double features his parents would take him to see as a boy. The ones with war propaganda reels before them, so to keep America's youth ready and willing to kill for the flag.

Leo's restlessness pries Kimberly from sleep. Her red hair passes beneath his nose as she stirs and plants herself on his bare chest and smiles in a way suggesting this is a pleasant surprise, as unexpected for her as it is for him.

She's been waiting here a long time.

"You're up early," she says and kisses his throat, then gives his stubble a playful suck.

It's good enough to make Leo stop thinking about his nights walking along blood-splattered sidewalks. Retreating through freezing shadows while wondering whether distant sirens are hunting him.

He isn't thinking about those young and wayward faces. How they all died the same way, expressions crystalized in disbelief.

None of that belongs to Leo anymore. In him now is another set of priorities. He closes his eyes and feels them settling across his fiber. Nesting like some trespassing animal. Lesson plans. Teacher conferences. Saturdays doing chores in the yard.

Today he's going downtown to the hardware shop to buy enough wood to start the deck. Winter has been unseasonably mild in the 'burbs and he wants to take advantage.

He doesn't destroy anymore. He creates. Families. Lessons. Wood decks. All the relationships that exist and form these connections. Steve at the hardware shop. He's got two kids in Tommy's school. One's ready for NYU in the fall. Other wants to stay behind and work the store. Learn the trade from his dad.

Nothing sounds better to Leo than this life. After ten years of being a ghost, he's returned to the land of the living.

Don't worry about that anymore, he tells himself. *You've won a second chance. Don't waste it.*

He knows he should get started on the day but pulls Kimberly close and wraps his arms around her, squeezing as if trying to absorb her body. She makes a few startled yips against his cheek and that only makes him cuddle harder. Last time he saw her, she was the color of death, lying flat on a slab of stainless steel.

"What are you doing?" Kimberly's wiggling around trying to get free. He loosens his arms so she'll stay put but he makes no motion to answer.

Freeze this moment, he thinks, then keeps hanging on.

4

BREAKFAST IS CLOSER TO LUNCH by the time they're eating.

Kimberly cooks bacon, eggs, and toast and she's wearing that kimono he bought her while on their honeymoon in Japan. Once in a while her thigh slips out from underneath the fabric and that unintended display of flesh, the thing he's not supposed to see in that moment, arouses and excites him.

She always did have a wonderful figure.

"The Boutwells are doing that potluck cookout tonight," Kimberly says, taking a bite of toast and using her pinkie to sweep a small crumb out of the corner of her mouth.

"Are we going?"

"I'm making five pounds of garlic chicken wings."

"I don't like what's-his-name," Leo says, unsure of why he's saying it, realizing his mind carries no knowledge of this offending what's-his-name.

"Joshua," she answers, seemingly all too aware of whatever their history is. "From down the street?"

"Joshua," Leo says. "Sounds about right." There's a picture in his head now. Joshua Gibson, originally from Boston, now of Manhasset Hills. Kind of guy who drops sports affiliations like a bad habit. No more Yaz or Bobby Orr in his life. Now he wears Yankee pinstripes.

Rangers red and blue.

No greater tell for people who can't be trusted. Easiest way to identify those who stand for nothing. Loyalty has to be deeper than an address.

"What about him?" Kimberly asks. "You're not going to stay home just because he's there, are you?"

Leo is still staring at that kimono, and he's thinking about how he once took a knife to the shoulder while pulling a mugger off a Japanese tourist, and how he had to pay a veterinarian to stitch him up at 2 a.m.

Never happened, Leo snaps. And then he can no longer remember what it is he's thinking about. A knife? Animals barking in a kennel? Arm being sewed?

Who knows. He needs to start getting more sleep at night.

Whatever that train of thought, it's gone now. Replaced by banal faculty dinners and chaperone duty on annual field trips to The Cloisters. A place he's never been.

You have, Leo. Every spring.

Across the table, Kimberly stares with a sweet, affecting smile, bite after bite of bacon. Nothing to say, just that grin spreading, widening, strangely disconnected from the situation.

Leo's own contented smile shrinks in response.

5

HE SHOWERS, THEN DRESSES. BLUE jeans. A brown tee that's a tight fit over his larger-than-average arms. One of the reasons he prefers doing yard work himself is to stay fit. Working in a classroom makes it too easy to wilt.

He wipes steam off the bathroom mirror and sees shattered glass. A half dozen Leos staring back. It isn't the first time he's seen them. Back in his hotel room—

What room? His thoughts are hostile now and he's no longer allowed to question his confusion.

One reflection is Leo Holland, domesticated house husband. Another instance is far more disquieting. Leo in a knitted black cap, face speckled with a stranger's blood. He feels connected to this shard, perhaps more than any other and is less enthused by the Leo looking in this bathroom with a faraway gaze and a Baretta pressed to his temple. Enough grief on his face to fill a funeral procession.

These images hang in the glass for a moment and then they're gone, replaced in full by Suburban Leo, who combs his hair while dismissing everything as a trick of the mind. But that's just what his brain is telling him: "Everything is fine!"

It's clear his thoughts have betrayed him.

Deep down it's a lie and he understands this. The taste of crisp bacon might haunt his throat just as the fresh ground coffee continues to energize him, that extra boost to go out and greet the day.

Somehow, though, it's all a lie.

"Honey," Kimberly says. One well-timed knock on the bathroom door to disrupt his current thinking. "Tommy stayed at Scotty's house last night and you'll have to pick him up before you go to the store."

"Okay," he says and opens up.

She gives him a soft pat on the butt as he passes and says, "I love you."

Leo turns toward her, about to say it back because it is the truth. But she's just standing there, frozen in her kimono, that same empty smile and those bright-but-vacant eyes. This confirms for him what he's already concluded.

It's a lie.

He scoops his keys off the kitchen table and tells himself everything's fine and well with the hope his hostile brain might believe him.

6

TOMMY AND HIS FRIEND SCOTTY are in the driveway drinking Cokes when Leo pulls in.

"Hey, Mr. Holland," Scotty says. "Nice to see you, sir."

It's been a long time since anyone has called Leo anything at all, let alone *Mr. Holland*. A name from another life.

This life?

Leo waves as Tommy climbs into the cab and all he can think is, *I haven't seen you in ten years.*

He catches himself in the rearview and bloodshot eyes stare back. A glossy raccoon bruise painted around one of them. He recalls getting into a fistfight on the subway, some junkie trying to boost every handbag on the train, nailing the patrolman with his pig sticker, leaving him leaking on the floor.

Would've gotten away had Leo not been there to pull a gun. Almost didn't matter. The guy came charging and their bodies tumbled out onto the station platform only for Leo to send him screaming to the third rail, body sparking and crisping as passengers retrieved their stolen bags and lauded him with hand shakes and thank yous.

Never happened.

Tommy looks at him with a sad smile. "Hey, Dad." Outside the cab, the sky darkens around them, the dream beginning to collapse.

"I'm sorry," Leo says. "I'm so sorry." This is his son, a young man now. A façade. Leo stares anyway, taking in the decade of living this figment has enjoyed. Sliding across a baseball diamond to Little League cheers. Sweaty hands gently touching a girl's hips—two seventh graders swaying along to Loggins and Messina. His first dance. All the personality that takes shape, forms a soul, in the time that was stolen away.

An imagined future he'll never get to see.

Tommy has no reaction to Leo's tears. Much like Kimberly in the bedroom, or at the breakfast table, there's only sadness. Nothing behind it.

A lie that's limited in scope because the hotel's only got access to Leo's mind. It doesn't know his wife and son from anything except his memories. And now he's reached the end of the demonstration and reality would like to have him back.

Leo blinks.

Then gags.

Sits up and winces. There's a foul taste on his tongue. His forehead strikes metal and he crashes back to the floor, eyes adjusting to the dark.

Ambient light surrounds him, bright enough to reveal openings on his left and right. Leo wiggles out onto a hotel room floor, free of the bed he's been wedged beneath. He opens his mouth, tongue pushing out the dark sludge that fills it. Onyx muck spills over his lips, a slow dribble down his chin.

"You're going to let me go," he growls, getting to his feet, leaning on the wall for breath and balance.

Only now does Leo realize there's someone sitting on top of the bed.

Unlike the blank face he'd seen earlier that had chased him into this dream, this one's a man in a wrinkled suit, head tucked into his hands. Motionless, smelling of cheap cologne. A lost soul, a former guest whose misery resonates as another echo, same as the girl who'd gone out the window.

"*Abyssinia, darling.*"

Grief lingers inside the Steinmann Hotel like stale cigarette smoke.

"Oh, but that's not all," Kimberly says and suddenly she's there too, right beside the entrance, still wearing that Japanese kimono, flashing her thigh as her leg lifts and stretches so her toes can touch the wall.

He's grown to regard her presence as a cruel trick.

GRAFFITI TOMBS

Kimberly's smile is wicked, observing her ex-husband with hatred. Her lips curl back and a rotted smile beams. Swollen gums. Maggots dancing on her tongue.

This is not his wife but a psychological weapon wielded against him.

"We have more to show you," she says and opens the door to reveal cold city streets where a dilapidated hallway is supposed to be. Thick wisps of swirling steam glide inward, flooding the room, filling it.

Kimberly gestures to the sidewalk like a gameshow host.

"You're going to want to see this one," she says.

"More lies."

"Nuh-uh."

He knows the only way out of here is to go through and he's come too far to do anything else.

So he steps out onto the cold city streets.

WORLD DESTRUCTION

1

THEY RIDE THE ELEVATOR TO twenty-one, which is as high as it goes, and Angela's as far away from Rake inside the car as she can get.

He's against the opposite wall. Head tilted back. Eyes closed. Hands by his sides, the gun in his fist pointed at the floor. He looks as though he's trying to accept a difficult loss or resolve some swirling conflict.

What she doesn't know is that Rake is combatting old urges that have returned. He's trying to ignore how much he'd like to bash her to death with a hammer, worried because maybe he isn't as strong as he thinks.

Maybe that's what the hotel wants to prove.

When the doors re-open, Rake makes no motion to move until Angela stirs.

"What did you see down there?" he asks.

"We were just trying to get out."

He tilts forward and looks possessed. "You looked like a desperate animal when I found you." There's enjoyment in the way he speaks to her. A kitten batting around a captured mouse.

Angela slides into the hall. Twenty-one is well-lit, and the stability of that light inspires a sense of irrational safety. She may still be in the Steinmann where every inch is a testament to human suffering, but the malevolence does not seem to exist up here. Maybe ghosts are afraid of heights.

Maybe they're scared of someone else.

"I asked you a question," Rake says once Angela's silence has stretched on for too long.

"You saw the stairwell."

"No, I didn't, but I guess that's the problem."

"I didn't see anything," Angela says. "The door swung closed. Ruben screamed."

"I gave you every chance in the world to be straight," he tells her. "Just remember that."

Angela knows what he wants to hear. How that trench coated thing dissected a woman before their eyes. She can tell by his face Sassoon is very important to him but knows better than to be the bearer of that news.

You just stood by and let it happen?

"You're safe up here," he says without trying to sell the lie. In Rake's mind, there's more to this story and he's wondering if maybe the script has flipped. Maybe The Man has sent some undercover cunt to bring him down. Sure is hard to gauge her, though, with her patched face and shitty, mismatched clothes.

The Man has never been this creative before.

Angela is drawn to a scrawl of red graffiti that says: THE BEACH FIXES EVERYTHING and the incongruity of this suggestion is unnerving. Who would write that here? For what purpose?

"It's strange," Rake says from behind, scratching his cheek with his gun barrel. "I was supposed to meet a girl down there and I find you instead. Shrieking like a banshee."

"This hotel isn't right," she says. "We all feel that."

"What do you feel?" He's looking at her as if he's desperate to have that question answered.

"It's the sort of thing that'll get you committed if you say it out loud."

"I'm not your fucking shrink so . . ."

"Best I can tell . . ." Angela realizes this is going to sound insane. "It amplifies your fears and insecurities, except . . . that's not exactly right because it also made me go for a swim in a flooded ballroom of human remains. So maybe, what I've come up with is that the hotel just gets off on tormenting us."

Rake doesn't want to hear this. It's the only conclusion a rational person can make. He waves the gun in Angela's face and she correctly intuits the gesture, starts walking the length of the hall. He moves alongside her with the barrel hovering against her ribs.

Where are you, Leo? Angela peels the gauze dressing off her hands and allows the bandage to fall. Rake is too distracted to notice as she stretches her palms to crack open the scabs there. Tiny drops of blood slide down the inside of her hand, plopping off her fingertips, leaving crimson breadcrumbs on the carpet.

"There you are." Rake is relieved to find the stairwell as it should be. Accessible. He opens the door to the landing and uses the gun to draw Angela's attention to the plywood sheets lining the slab floor.

"Hey, this is great, if we can go down from here—"

"It's just us now," Rake says and performs a hot step diagonal from the doorway to the ascending steps. Then he whirls around with surprising agility, pointing the gun at her head. "Follow me exactly or we're both dead."

The boards are there to mask his array of Soviet anti-personnel mines that he bought off some white supremacist in Brooklyn. A fat fuck always barking about the upcoming race war to anyone who'll listen. Rake pities his ignorant ass 'cause he's too stupid to see the real game. That the scumbags in power use pawns like him to keep everyone entrenched in old thinking. Make the little people hate each other so they don't notice they're trapped in the belly of a dying beast.

Rake didn't ask for this awareness. He just has it. All he's gotta do is live a few more hours to turn the pillars of heaven to dust, send the cloud of *haves* crashing back down into the world of *have nots*.

Angela follows Rake as he climbs, blood dribbling down her fingers, suggesting a safe path for anyone who might follow. She repeats the process on every landing until they reach twenty-three and from there it's just a short walk.

"Step slow, hear me?" Rake says as he unlocks the room that is their destination.

A thin rope stretches across the floor there. Rake takes an exaggerated step over for her benefit. Angela clocks it, then follows. To her right, past the bathroom where the room opens wider, is a shotgun bolted to the wall. The rope is attached to the trigger, primed to blast anyone who trips it.

"Home defense," he tells her, then begins to climb the aluminum ladder in the center of the room that extends up through a manmade hole in the ceiling. "Move your ass."

Angela follows, knowing better than to trust him, but where can she run? What other traps has he hidden around here? It's him or the hotel and at least she knows how to handle men. And if Leo's still alive, this is the son of a bitch he's gunning for.

She's done everything she can to lead him along.

She climbs up and Rake is leaning against the wall surrounded by bricks of cocaine. He's got a real prideful grin about showing off his inner sanctum. "King of the city," he says. "You like?"

"Does Your Majesty happen to have a phone?"

Her dismissal is disappointing. Or she's got one hell of a poker face because it's part of her job. Turbo had warned of "some guy" asking questions in the lobby, though it isn't beyond Vice to try their luck with a rookie whore.

He takes her chin in his hand and squeezes her cheeks, studying her face and then her body, smirking all the way down as he fantasizes about breaking her in. If she is Vice, it would be fun to see how deep her cover goes because that's the thing about nine-to-fivers: They all got husbands and kids but sometimes they're so dedicated to the job they're willing to embrace degeneracy to sell their cover. It's a huge turn on—the extra degradation—and this one looks committed to the bit. It'd be fun to put her to work.

"I love a bitch with a smart mouth," he says. "A bitch who talks shit. I bet you can talk some shit."

"I, uh, don't know," she says and eases from his grip, gliding toward the phone with the slightest sashay of her hips to suggest maybe she can be a good sport. "May I talk to the front desk—?"

"Try your luck."

She does and it's kaput. Tosses the receiver down.

"Before I got cut off from the mainland, my guy downstairs told me some things were in motion."

Angela's poker face flinches but holds. One thing she's invaluably good at. An intractable requirement of her job. Never allow your clients to know what you're thinking. You may walk into a house to find a cracked-out mom hallucinating, feces in a bucket, malnourished kids who look like skeletons, and it doesn't matter. Gotta have a steady hand or you risk making things worse.

She learned long ago to be unflappable. To keep a steady breath and a clear head, because it can be the difference between life and death. It's already been that way for her more times than she should have to know.

It is again today.

Rake lifts his gun and looks it over. A kind of vague threat. "Somebody's running around this hotel looking for me," he says. "All you gotta do is tell me about him."

"Ruben." She's committed to his name because it's easier to sell a half-truth than a total lie. "Uh, he's just a kid that works here. I did tell you about him . . . Back on ten? The guy I was trying to save."

The gun barrel is staring her down again, one wide eye ready for action. "Who else?"

"I was here to check on a family, okay? That's my job. Then I'm climbing up a dumbwaiter and someone's trying to stab me. Ruben pulled me out. Ruben's who I know."

Rake doesn't have the same poker face and his smirking urge to blast a hole through her forehead cannot hide the fact Angela's story continues to disturb him. Somebody from the outside and on the up and up—not a hallucinating junkie—confirming his newfound suspicion. Something is wrong in this hotel and it always has been.

Let's see how wrong it is.

He lifts his gun toward the ceiling, turning the heat down on Angela. She takes a breath now that the barrel's pointed elsewhere. He uses the pistol to gesture to the door and she goes with a slow shuffle.

It's a short walk across the hall to 2403, which is unlocked. Rake pushes open the door and steps aside. "Welcome to the historic Steinmann Hotel. Enjoy your stay."

The darkness there makes Angela think of walking into the mouth of some prehistoric creature. To cross this threshold is to slide willingly into her own demise. "Please don't make me—"

"Shut the fuck up."

Being alone in here induces a panic she's never felt. She shakes and pleads. "Can't I stay with you?" She really doesn't want that but maybe if he believes it . . .

"No."

"If you leave me in here, I'll die."

Rake trains the gun on her as he reverses into the hall, door closing in slow motion, sweeping away the last vestiges of light. "Yeah," he says, "that's what I'm curious about." And then he's gone.

Angela could try to follow him out, knowing full well that would result in a bullet to the face. She goes to the phone out of reflex and almost doesn't bother, but old habits bring her hand down on the receiver anyway. This time there are voices in mid-conversation. "I'm telling you there's something outside," one says. "In the hallway."

"*Something?*"

"Don't you hear it?"

"It's laughter," a voice on the phone suggests.

Except it isn't. It's a humorless sound much closer to an animal's instinct. A hyena howl or something worse. Maybe a creature that knows to copy human emotion without understanding it.

"Are you going to come up and check?" the voice asks.

"This is the second night you've called."

"This is the second night it's happened. What kind of place are you running?"

"On my way."

The line clicks dead. Before Angela can place the receiver down, the phone rings again and another voice says, "Front desk."

"Hey," the voice is already agitated. "We're in 2403 and—"

Constant knocking overpowers the conversation.

Angela grips the phone as the thumps get louder and, in a split second, make the jump from the phone line into the hallway outside.

Angela screams and the phone goes silent, tumbling out of her hand.

The knocking has found her. That same impatient barrage that had pounded from behind every door on the third floor has suddenly resurfaced, looking to have a word.

"What do you want?" she screams, hoping the man who brought her here might come running.

He brought you here for this.

At her feet, the phone barks, demanding to be placed back on its cradle. The impatient dial tone like an air siren. It startles Angela and forces the knocker in the hall to go quiet for a long moment.

Until the front door pushes open and catches on the lock chain Angela hadn't set. A blade glides into the space there. Shimmering bloodstains along the steel like grape jam on morning toast. The knife pushes on the chain, a gentle *tink tink* each time it touches, trying to clear it away.

The phone ceases its repetitive wail and cedes to a different voice suddenly calling up to Angela, asking, "Hello? Hello?" with wobbly repetition.

The blade is still working the chain and Angela bends to the floor without taking her eyes off it. She feels around for the receiver, fingers finding purchase, picking it up. "Yes? Are you there?"

"I have a message for you," the voice says. "You're not going to like it. You're going to die up there."

The knife taps the chain as if to underscore that declaration. The caller and the killer working in tandem.

Angela slips her hand inside her pants pocket, fingers sheathing brass knuckles once more. *Fine*, she thinks, remembering the lesson she had to learn back home. The one lesson her life is never going to allow her to forget.

Fight.

The knife continues tapping the chain. Repetition is the point. It's never going to get inside this way, but that's not what this is about. It's about stoking her fear. Angela's jaw swivels back and forth as she gathers her strength, giving her body over to the adrenaline high that's demanding to drive.

"Okay," she says and charges, throwing her shoulder into the door so it slots back into place. From the hall, a startled body leaps away in surprise and Angela feels it's time to go on offense. She slides the chain from its slot and it's dangling down, clacking against the door as she tears it open and rushes into—

An empty hall.

"It's fear," she says, looking to her left and then her right. Fear is how this hotel hurts you. She knows a thing or two about fear. Her entire childhood is a monument to it. At its base, a father. A failure. A man so miserable he chose to take his aggression out on the only two people who loved him.

She's smelling those cheapo cigars again because the hotel knows all about the Hav-A-Tampas.

"It won't work," she says. Angela survived those years by locating the strength inside herself and fortifying it.

Tonight she's exhausted. Blood-crusted and battered. "Still alive," she spits in defiance because that part bears repeating. Still alive. Her fear is shifting, transforming into something else because fear is a choice.

One she chooses to reject.

"That's how you beat this," she says, looking around the hallway, almost daring the hotel to attack.

And when the Steinmann decides to hold back, she starts off to find the man who brought her here.

2

RAKE IS JUST OUTSIDE THE last room on the right, tuned to Angela's footsteps as she rounds the corner. The anxiety on her face talking loud and clear.

"What is it?" he asks like an excited boy. "What did you see?"

"You already know."

"Tell me what happened."

She's ready to talk, eager to demand answers to her questions, when a tangle of muffled groans comes out of the room beside them, shifting the dynamic and forcing a pall over their conversation.

Angela's attention glides to the open doorway where the sudden emergence of inhuman cries is louder.

"Shut up," Rake snaps toward the black of the room, doesn't want it interrupting Angela. She's emerged from her cocoon with a coolness difficult for him to process. Her fear, exorcised and traded for determination. She did more than face it down. She came out ready for more.

"Who is that?" she asks of the whimpers, unable to hide her distress, fearful it could be Ruben or Leo in there crying out in agony. And though she's found her strength, it is a fleeting supply that can be depleted should events shift out of her favor.

"What did you see?" Rake barks.

The room is calling to Angela, pulling her toward it. Rake slides into her path and lifts a backhand to her face.

Angela slips between his shoulder and the jamb. Once she's inside, she takes a sharp turn to the right and looks down on the bathroom floor where a powdered brick has been sliced open on the cold tile. A mess of a man is feeding off it like a starved mongrel, huffing and cackling behind every snort like he's really getting away with something.

"Oh my God."

The addict catches shifting light in his peripheral and looks up. His eyes are like fried eggs and a mischievous giggle vibrates in his throat. He regards Angela with a shrug, then goes back to snorting because nothing matters more than this free junk buffet.

"Die!" Rake screams as he pushes Angela aside, kicking the addict in the face, sending him back against the toilet, ribs cracking. He simply giggles and comes crawling back toward the brick. "Why is he alive?" Rake is looking to Angela for an explanation, the soft curiosity of a boy asking his mother about the world.

"I d-d-don't . . ." Angela cannot answer this, stuttering like a skipping record.

"Doesn't make any sense, does it?" Rake says. "See, I thought I was evolving up here, but if it's been the hotel this whole time, then what the hell am I? No better than this piece of shit. That's what."

Angela can only shrug. There's no talking people off some ledges.

"This place is thriving off his addiction and misery," Rake says, "using it like a tank of diesel unleaded." The greater horror in this moment is existential. The idea that Rake isn't a god of anything, simply another cog in the hotel's wheel.

What if he's never been in charge of his own destiny? Just a different kind of puppet—same as every other miserable bastard in this dive.

That's a difficult thing for a god to reconcile.

You didn't think you were special, did you? A god? You've always been a loser.

Without the Burnt Book and the hotel's guidance, Rake is little more than another failed artist and suddenly he's longing for his trusty claw hammer—the paint brush with which he rearranges women's faces.

No.

That's what he would've been without coming here. The Steinmann helped him to realize his potential.

If you say so.

"Shut up," Rake growls.

Angela is trying to resist her bleeding-heart urge to roll up her sleeves, get down on her knees and help this poor man, but he's too far gone and the best thing for him is that she survives this ordeal. Someone has to call for help and if she doesn't get out, nobody may ever know he's here.

"Know what?" Rake says, cruelty snapping back into place as he points a finger at his prisoner, The Package. "Snort up, fucker. It all ends at daylight." He's back to watching Angela with broader curiosity, eager to hear her answer. What did the hotel throw at her? How is she holding it together when he's on the verge of coming apart?

It's Angela's turn to reverse-walk into the hall, the grim resolve of Rake's statement pushing her to retreat. He's told her very little, though his behavior has explained it all. She was never leaving this floor alive.

Rake snatches her arm because he's suddenly got all sorts of bad thoughts sifting through his brain. If he can't be a god, if that was all just pillow talk between he and the hotel, then he might as well enjoy himself. One last installation to pass the time. Urges the Steinmann has suppressed for a while, helping him to pursue something greater.

Something he really believed had come from him and him alone.

It's two birds with one stone, because that coward vigilante is sure to come calling and even better.

"I'm not finished with you," he says. "We're waiting for one more. And we both know it ain't Ruben."

Except he is finished. Angela cracks him in the face, brass to cheek. His eyes ignite and he punches her in reflex, knuckles crashing into her mouth, re-opening the knife wound there. A warm rush of blood spreads across the gauze pad fastened to her face and her tongue's alive with the taste of metal.

She smashes into the opposite wall and pushes off, roaring and aiming those knuckles at his nose. A cookie crunch as she connects. Rake goes staggering into the room where Georgie, more animal than man at this point, giggles excitedly at the sight of his tormentor doing a pratfall over the bed.

Angela dashes for those glowing red letters—E-X-I-T—and Rake is running too, his disgusting breath spilling across her neck as he grabs for her, fingers catching the fabric of her Steinmann Hotel shirt, then slipping away.

She's light-headed from pushing so hard, her mind repeating one newfound mantra over and over: *Fear is a choice. Fear is the killer.*

She remembers what it was like to be a frightened little girl. Terrified of Daddy coming home. Praying he wouldn't be in a bad mood for once. That he wouldn't take his anger out on her. As if she'd done a single thing to earn his wrath. She was a child whose biggest concern had been how many imaginary friends would be joining her for tea and crumpets. Jiminy Cricket was always a no show.

This hotel is not unlike her dad. They smell roughly the same, for starters—the fragrance of spilt beer and cigarette smoke around every corner—and the harder it fights to feast on her, the more she rejects it.

When you're a survivor, you don't know how to do anything but.

It's why she came to the city. Maybe she was running, but she was also challenging herself. *Go somewhere that needs your help and help.* Prove to others anyone can have a life because you can.

In a twisted way, Angela's entire existence has prepared her for this miserable stay in the Steinmann.

Rake screams from somewhere. His words are mush. She glances back and the lower half of his face is slathered in blood that won't stop gushing from busted nostrils.

She pushes through the door to reach the landing and is careful to move along the same diagonal pattern to the stairs leading up.

Something shoves her against the wall. The blow snatches all the wind from her lungs, making it impossible to react to the thing she's seeing. The man whose fingers are closing around her neck.

She's back to wondering why Jiminy Cricket never makes it to her parties because, suddenly, she's face-to-face with her father.

The man she killed five years ago.

IT'S THE SPIRAL

1

YOU'RE HAVING A 42ND STREET dream.

The city, a blur of bustling lights. Blinking bulbs of red and green. Sirens scream in the distance because it's always someone's turn to have a tragedy.

Look down that alley. See the junkie shooting shit straight into his blood? Good. Watch his eyes roll back, mouth drape open. Would you believe this is the best night of his life?

The brain isn't as smart as we think. Synthetic bliss is good enough. And what's the harm? With a life this bad, can you really blame him?

Everybody's got habits. You do, don't you?

Blam

Blam

Blam

Blam

Blam

Blam

Blam

Blam

Blam

Blam

Blam

GRAFFITI TOMBS

Blam

Click.

Reload.

We know how to fix this, Leo. Junkies like this. Send them away. Well, what does 'away' mean? Put them someplace. Oh, you mean jail. "For the good of society," yeah? And too bad for their loved ones, of course.

Hear that screaming baby? Hang on, wait for the siren to go away. Okay, there. You hear it? A common sound in these parts—like an owl on a country road. Take that kid away from his mom who just got high, whose cheeks are numb and who desperately needs an escape from the harsh realities of her life.

Not everybody can afford a plane ticket to the Bahamas.

Hey, there's programs, right? Social workers who "care." No, don't worry about Angela right now, Leo. You cannot afford to worry about Angela. Maybe she does want to help—you as well as them—but it's too late for any of that.

You're going to want to see this, my man.

We're back on that junkie in the alleyway who's staring up at the moon, numb from a face-full of pins and needles. A good nod taking hold.

He was born Louis Robert Tommlinson and he grew up hard in some Long Island town. Like most of the people you've plugged, he wasn't born bad, okay? Lost his father in Korea, which made his mom get hooked on Mother's Little Helper and then—

No, we're not making excuses. The world is more complex than "excuses" and what you need to know is that Louis Robert Tommlinson caught a bad shake. Had to grow up alone. Fell in with a crew, kind of guys who didn't only know they were gonna die young, but couldn't wait to do it.

He's boosting cars and peddling smack for the guineas in Jersey before his fourteenth birthday 'cause you need to be honest with yourself, Leo. It always goes back to men in suits, but you can't shoot that far, can you? You settle for the strays in your backyard. What you hunt is cannon fodder.

A kid like Louis is clay. He gets molded into a weapon during those revolving door stints at juvie centers up and down the eastern seaboard. They tell him he's there 'cause he's no good and if he wants to stay out, he's gotta be smarter.

Know what that does to a mind? *"You're no good. You're a problem."*

Especially when you're a child whose foundations have crumbled to dust and are replaced by the cold, clinical support of state systems? Your name as a number? Little more than processed food on an assembly line.

It's no one's fault, really, everyone's doing the best they can to fix the clogged drain. That's what makes it all so messy.

You catch a deal like Louis Robert Tommlinson's and you're always playing defense. Always looking for trouble. So much trouble you stick some kid in the guts 'cause he looks at you wrong and the only thing you know about the world is it's kill or be killed and life seems cheaper than a half of whiskey.

Louis does five years in Sing Sing for that. The judge looks at his jacket and figures a sentence like that will put hair on his chest. Give him plenty of time to think about what he's done.

Know what he learns instead?

How to survive. How to become a hard man. He falls in with a crew and it's gotta be Nazis 'cause he's a white dude and nobody else is gonna talk to his ass even though he's never had much of a problem with other colors.

He thinks about the black kid across the street from him growing up. Chester Washington. They used to play stickball before dinner and in a lot of ways it was the happiest Louis had ever been.

Some nights, he wonders what happened to him.

But now he's got a swastika over his heart to amplify the hatred beating inside of him. He hates this world and everyone in it. He beats a black man blind because his tribe needs to make sure he's got the anger. Later, he shanks one of his own for informing.

That's just the beginning. Before he can even wonder how he got here, he's hurling a Molotov at that one guard the entire block hates. And everyone's laughing as they watch him burn, body twisting around in panic, turning into Rice Krispies, snap, crackle, popping.

It's during his stay in Sing Sing that he stops going by Louis Robert Tommlinson, and there would come a point later in life where he doesn't even remember his birth name. He's Torch now and he discovers it's kind of cool to have a name that reflects what he loves: Watching things burn.

Torch does his five years, then gets out. They never managed to pin any of that shit on him 'cause no one on the inside talks without taking a shiv to their heart. It barely matters because all he needs to do to fool The Man is keep on showing up to work. License plates.

He's there every day, always productive. Gold star. Attendance on a sheet. The state reads it and thinks he's rehabbed. It gets to pat itself on the back for that accomplishment and receive a reward from Uncle Sam. Fed bucks. Only thing that matters.

Never once does Torch consider changing his ways. It's been so long his ways are all he knows. In '74 he's back on the street at twenty-three. Never returns to Long Island 'cause his mom overdosed while he was inside. The house sold and who needs those memories anyway? They ain't so great.

He's barely a man. Humanity got peeled away in strips on the inside and now he's more like a bundle of raw nerves. Primal instinct. His goal each morning is to survive and he greets each day like he's walking into a street fight.

He cuts through people like wet paper, taking what he needs. He's got connections all over the borough, guys who will pay cash for whatever he can score.

Here's where you come in, Leo.

See that bitch across the street? The redhead in the forty-dollar coat, holding that little kid's hand? They ain't even in the wrong part of town. Wasn't like people traipsing through the East Village past crumbling tenements and stripped cars, hordes of homeless on The Bowery . . . you sorta know what you're getting into if that's where you're headed.

This was Brooklyn, and Mom and Child are ascending out of the subway after a day at the Bronx Zoo, hurrying home before the streets get even darker.

Torch sees them coming.

He isn't thinking about the man they've got at home. He doesn't care about you at all.

They're a walking payday. The purse swaying off her elbow is a pendulum and Torch is hypnotized by every glint of that handbag's golden latch as it swings beneath streetlamps. Might as well be dollar signs and—

No, you've got to watch this, Leo.

With this score, Torch can finally think about getting his own place. Get the hell out of that shelter because he can't stand the oily gruel they call stew. This score is important and he tells himself he's always been a businessman and that's what he'll do. Start slinging pussy and smack instead of wasting all his money on it.

All these guys have the same American Dream.

The redhead sees him coming. He can tell by the way she stiffens, pulling that stupid kid close to her body as Torch crosses the street, grinning like a shark, unable to hide his intentions because he doesn't care to.

She's nothing to him. Less than zero, Leo, if you want the truth. You really should understand the *hows* and the *whys* that brought you here.

"Can I talk to you?" Torch says in a way that sounds like, "Stick 'em up, bitch." She's already shrieking and that's before he pulls the gun. Tears it out of his pants and steps to her, shoving her into the alley she just so happens to be in front of.

Little Tommy's shrieking, rushing to her side.

Torch orders her to take it all off, except be careful with that fucking Macy's coat 'cause he's not paying to have it dry cleaned. Hand that over nice and slow, then get to work on your jewelry.

Ready for the kicker, Leo? She did everything right. I know you never blamed her but Kimberly was smart. No heroics.

Tommy throws himself against his mother's hips like he's trying to crawl back inside her womb and hide from the monster swinging the gun around.

Torch can't even say why it happened. He's been up for two days, tweaked, too withdrawn to sleep, too desperate for his next payout. People as slot machines.

Here's the way he remembers it: Her bag at his feet. She's fishing the watch off her wrist. He wants her rings too and she's not going to protest. She's got them all in her palm, all except that diamond, which is sparkling brighter than the skyline.

It's that sparkle . . . it plays tricks.

The diamond conjures shadows, and the gaps in his junkie brain happen to project the idea this bitch is doing something stupid . . . making a sudden move.

Torch never was as cool under pressure as he thought.

First shot is almost involuntary. He blasts her in the chest and her body explodes. He's never seen one buckle and break like that. The sound of shattering bone and a blood splatter that's closer to a flood.

She tumbles and falls onto her back and her eyes are wild now because her greatest fear has happened, she's shot and dying and reaching for her child, one last desperate act, to push his body out of harm's way.

Torch doesn't even know why he does what he did next.

He could've just cut and run. But the boy's shrieks are loud enough to bring the weight of the world down on him and when you're suffering from the disease, you do what it takes to grin and bear it.

It happens fast. Torch sights the banshee kid down the barrel and shoots him in the face. The gun barks and blows his jaw clean off. Kid who ain't even ten goes spinning through the air and lands motionless on a bed of flattened cardboard, the most fucked up gurgle in his throat, weird twitches, 'cause little kids aren't supposed to die like that.

None of it can be stopped now.

Torch shoots the mom again and this bullet's a Medusa gaze that turns her to stone.

Worst part? There's blood all over that Macy's coat. Fuckin' worthless now.

He collects it anyway, along with everything else, and runs faster than he ever has, taking train after train, refusing to stop until he's uptown where the unbroken stream of taxicab songs—honk, honk, honk—help him to relax. He never forgets that night, though. Only time he's ever felt guilt.

Not enough to change, of course. Torch keeps running, drowning inside waves of chemical highs meant to chase away the bad dreams. They're cropping up with much more frequency now.

He never learns about the monster he created that night, either.

Across town, you, Leo Holland, are getting the call and you're processing your grief with immediate thoughts of murder. Payback. Almost no time passes between then and your nights on the town, hunting men like Torch, shooting them dead—many for far less, but so what, right? So long as you feel in control again.

What I can tell you is that Torch heard stories of the vigilante. He even knew one of guys you clipped, but the whole of it is beyond him. The plague of death unleashed upon his kind as a result of his own actions? Come on. That's not the kind of thing a man like Torch ever takes stock of. Introspection is for the privileged.

That's the thing about this. Crime is not a vicious circle. It's a spiral. It didn't start with Torch. He got caught in it, same as you, and you're both on downward spins, crimes carrying consequences beyond your intentions.

Torch created Leo the vigilante, but what did you create?

Oh, you want to know how I know all this? Well, that's the best part. One night, Torch checked in to the Steinmann eager for peace and quiet so to enjoy his high. Couldn't take all the snoring and the farting that scores the shelter. Anyway, while he was here, he had the worst dreams of his life, Kimberly and Tommy on a loop. A movie reel spinning forever across the screen in his brain.

He woke the next day unrested and even more disturbed. We might have lost track of him once he pushed out through the front door that morning, but he did leave a piece of his soul behind. And if we do anything here at the Steinmann, it's sifting through misery and sorrow for all those fascinating nuggets.

We make connections, Leo. We link his thoughts to yours and now at least you have some closure.

Or do you?

On that, Leo sees something swirling through the sonorous void. Little whips of color that stain the darkness like streaks from a paint-brush, giving form to a man suddenly standing across from him. A man who looks down at his own dripping hand, watching as he's rec-reated out of nonexistence.

The paint or plaster or whatever it is that gives him life bleeds down over a human nose and parting lips, but the head holds two empty eye sockets and he looks less like a man, more like an animated Halloween mask.

Leo squints through those holes to the back of his rubber head, accessing the thoughts materializing there. They flicker like a peep show screen—seventy-five cents for ninety seconds. There's only one reel looping over and over: The one time this man shot a child in the face.

"I was gone," the plaster face says, distress rising through his voice. With only his upper body realized, phantom brush strokes con-tinuing to render his lower extremities in real time, this abomination, the thing that had once been Torch, tilts his head back to scream and a rush of plaster drips off his face and splatters across the black floor.

2

LEO STANDS OVER A BED where there's a figure tucked beneath the sheets. The man who murdered his family sleeping peacefully.

It's the peace that breaks him, that this man should have any. He shoots him through the head while he's in dreamland and his brains splatter across the headboard, into which the word LOVE is carved twice.

It's over.

He thinks about Kimberly and Tommy while staring at the immobile lump of bloodstained sheets and feels nothing for his efforts. No catharsis is possible and the sun continues rising as it has every day these last ten years. Nothing has changed outside or in.

Leo even forgets to cross himself, only now feeling the weight of hypocrisy the gesture carries for someone like him.

Leo Holland often thinks about how he died a long time ago, and how the world he inhabits, this city, is his tomb.

Torch lifts his splattered head off the pillow, face reanimated. He smiles as a hunk of brain pops out of the fresh-blown hole in his skull. "Not everything can be said." His voice is slow and monotonous, like a thing from another world attempting to translate its tongue into ours before speaking.

"Are you still alive?" Leo says. "In the world?"

The dead man shakes his head, seems terrified of this answer. "He does not know."

"Louis Robert Tommlinson," Leo says, committing the name and his blood-soaked face to memory.

The man smiles while blood streams out of his ears. As he sits up, a fresh pour of crimson glides smoothly down his cheek. "Going to find him?"

Leo barely hears the question, stands shivering in the void.

Torch flings the sheet aside and stands up. As soon as he's on his feet, the bed is gone and now it's just two men standing in the middle of nowhere. "There is more," he tells him. "All of what you don't want to know."

3

IT'S THE SPIRAL.

Remember the first mugger? The one you bashed off the side of the mouth with a roll of quarters?

Did you know he had a dying mother? Did you know that when he didn't come home, she got evicted? An Italian immigrant in her eighties who barely spoke English, whose cancer was eating her to the bone?

What kind of hero do you think you are, exactly?

As I was saying, Torch isn't the only one who contributed to the spiral. You're just as selfish. None of this has anything to do with justice. Certainly not now. The fire inside you rages and you're desperate to keep it lit, right? I mean, what happens if it goes out?

Leo watches himself move through a crowd of spiked hair and mohawks, torn tee shirts and people in dog collars moshing around broken beer bottles, casting middle fingers at the stage. The performers there are men in make-up and garter belts, screaming over toneless guitars about the world's destruction.

Leo has the Baretta in his fist, that greasy stagehand in his sights, because his kink is getting thirteen-year-old girls to pass out on the backstage couch.

Someone yells, "Fuck off, old man!" but they notice his gun and step back with a gasp that somehow slices through the grating music which is so loud it feels like a power drill at the back of Leo's head, detonating pain all the way to the front of his fillings. It really is hell on Earth here.

The pedophile knows the grim reaper is after him and trips over his fat feet, spilling to the floor. The crowd breaks around him with cruel and spiteful laugher that pinballs. Leo keeps walking, gun drawn.

Someone lunges for the Baretta, a kid whose shirt reads "FEAR" and who's ninety pounds soaking wet. Leo elbows him back into the crowd as the pervert scrambles to his feet.

Even the bouncer knows better than to get involved because everyone's heard of the vigilante. He's more than some urban legend and if you see him coming, it's best to go the other way.

It isn't the killing Leo needs to be reminded of. He knows this night, as brazen as he'd ever been, shooting the pervert in the back, once through the shoulder, and again through the heart in a roomful of witnesses.

He watches the man bowl forward, arms overhead as he crashes onto the same couch where he likes to do his business.

Everyone backstage scatters, screaming and shrieking because now they know who's visiting and nobody wants to be guilty by association. But here's the thing Leo doesn't realize: The pervert is always on his best behavior on Wednesdays. No drugs. No prowling. The straight and narrow.

Why?

Because his daughter is with him on Wednesdays. Twelve years old and locked away in the seclusion of the upstairs office. She happens to be looking out on the floor from that window, drawn to the commotion. And you can say she's better off. That's what you would've argued, at least, had you known. But she doesn't know her daddy's a creep. He doesn't prowl his own nest.

To her, some man stormed in and blasted him to death. And in the chaos, she's running toward his corpse, kneeling over his body in time to catch the life leaving him once and for all. Her innocence, stolen in a flash.

Should he be dead? Yeah, maybe. But look at the problem you created. Like many bad situations, answers are difficult to come by and often require something like a deft touch. That's the point.

Just the start of her problems because it's all pretty common now, right? Round and round, further down the spiral.

It gets worse for that kid. Her mom can't hack the full-time responsibilities of parenthood. Especially not with a newly trauma-tized daughter who wakes up screaming at night because the last thoughts of her father are of seeing his chest get blown open.

There's therapy, sure, but soon it's clear the only way to "resolve" this is through medication. And that doesn't deal with the problem. Just mutes it.

It's too much stress on Mom, who has no choice but to commit the girl to full-time care. Maybe she never would've had a chance at a normal life, but you did not help things, Leo. Not where she's con-cerned.

So how does this square with you? Prevent a couple of would-be victims while creating another?

This is how it goes. You meet every problem with a sledgehammer solution. And you're able to live with yourself because you're always fleeing the scene. Head on your pillow before the problems you cre-ate have a chance to take shape.

Down the spiral, round and round.

The daughter's out there, you know. Terrified of making connec-tions because she's positive she'll lose everyone in her life the way she lost her father. She's got nightmares of that man in the knitted cap weaving through the crowd and guess what she thinks?

She thinks he's coming back to kill her one of these days.

You think you're a good guy. Nothing to the contrary has ever crossed your mind. But you're as nasty as those you hunt. If there's any difference between you and the man upstairs you're so desperate to kill, it's that he's honest about his station.

Where is he, you ask? After all this, you're still eager to do it, huh? We need him here, Leo.

Look, you know about the mother you doomed to die, cold and alone in an alleyway, not unlike the resting place of your wife and son. And now you've heard about the daughter whose life you stole be-cause your destructive impulses are beyond control.

But what about the killer you created yourself? You mean you don't know? Guess you're more like Torch than maybe you realize, mutual ignorance of the destruction you little rascals unleashed.

I'm talking about the wife who never knew her husband was sup-plementing his family's income by peddling hash out the passenger side of his Datsun. She thinks he was the victim of a petty street crime when it was you who blasted his brains out through his ear. And it took some time, but now she's your exact copy, Vigilante Man.

Hunting a different borough every night of the week because it's the only thing that makes her feel alive anymore.

It's a spiral, man. Always spinning and expanding. An eternal pattern, ever-growing.

4

LEO SNAPS BACK TO IT with a shiver and the wind gusts are cold enough to take away his breath, his throat scraping as he reorients to whatever passes for reality inside the Steinmann.

He leans against the building and his boots are halfway off the window ledge, body locking up in the howling void, wind that doesn't just pass through but shoves him around. He wilts in the absence of light, both inside and out, but instinct is driving him back inside.

The Steinmann figured it would make things easy for him, but Leo isn't about to jump any more than he's willing to shoot himself. He's too stubborn for that, which the hotel both resents and admires.

He's got the Baretta in his fist and takes aim at the window next to him, firing one shot. It punches through the glass and he uses his boot to clear the pane of all the shards and then he slips inside.

It's warmer in here. The heat takes the chill from his bones. He tosses his weapon through the window and it goes spinning through the void because it's of no use where he's going and he can feel the hotel reacting to this surprising display.

The man who stepped in off that ledge isn't Leo Holland the vigilante but someone else.

Maybe life is a spiral, but Leo is not ready to risk letting any more of that poison hit the street. How wide does the spiral get should that happen? The hotel doesn't want to answer that question, because the hotel wants the world to suffer Rake's plague.

The hotel, Leo figures, was the architect—at least in part. A collaboration between an eager mind and these corrupted walls. This den of hatred finding a way to reach out and make the rest of the world hurt just as much as the tainted lifeforce dwelling here.

Should Leo destroy this pipeline, somebody worse will arise to restart it eventually because the spiral never stops. That's just life and he's learned to accept it.

But he's still going to slow it down.

Maybe everything the Steinmann has shown him is true. At least from a certain point of view. That's all the truth is anyway. He's no hero. Or even a good man and if he ever thought he was, Leo dropped that charade a million years ago. Doesn't mean he can't still do something good, though.

The hotel is furious, enraged the vigilante has resisted its efforts to force his surrender. Turns out guilt is as ineffective as the Steinmann's suburban artifice, the place it had expected him to remain cocooned.

The hotel laughs at this futility and the sound follows Leo out of the room and toward the elevator. It isn't the vigilante who's looking to reach twenty-one. The vigilante is spinning in oblivion with the Baretta that created a hundred more problems than this city ever needed.

This man is someone new. Leo reborn, not as a teacher, nor as a killer, but a man looking to resolve things in a way he never has.

"A concerned citizen," he quips in a bit of defiance the hotel does not appreciate. Negative energy pulsing around him.

The laughter is not one singular voice, but a chorus. Every bit of residual energy the hotel has, mocking him in stereo. It isn't the spirits this time but the Steinmann itself.

Laughing.

FRONT TOWARD
ENEMY

1

DIAGONALS. **ANGELA PUSHES TO REMEMBER** that as her watery eyes fall across the plywood boards covering the ground. *He sets the mines in diagonals.* That's been the pattern so far, and though she hasn't yet been to the twenty-fourth landing, she wants to believe her captor is a creature of habit.

The hand below her chin continues its squeeze on Angela's throat. Bone white and with hunks of blackened flesh clinging to it like a picked over buffalo wing. The leering face is ground hamburger, a cavernous recession where its eye and nose should be, the rest of its features sloping toward that large hole.

The smell should be fetid. Instead the air is staler than disco, dominated by Dominican leaves and cheap-ass tobacco. A step down from even the Hav-A-Tampas as she remembers what Dad was smoking on the day he died.

"You should never have left home," the man she called Dad growls, his words like slush, but still possessing a spitefulness that stirs a hundred memories Angela would rather forget.

How she was supposed to be running carefree around her yard in that dime store Snow White dress that Mom had picked out on her fifth birthday. How her greatest concern should've been teatime with seven magical friends, and that one damn cricket who was always too busy to come.

Instead, the most familiar sound of her childhood was that of Mom closing the bedroom door to cry in private and then, later, like clockwork, a trip to the bathroom to paint over her bruises.

Repetition. Kids understand routine more than anyone, though too often people mistake their pliability for invulnerability. Just because children can adapt to nightmares doesn't mean they should have to live them. Little Angela grows up thinking every kid's got a mean dad. It's how it is.

The man you believe is supposed to protect you but puts his fists on you instead, makes it hurt and forces you to live with the terror of *when*. Constant anxiety, a rat's nest at the front of her brain, overriding childhood innocence.

Fear is a choice. That comes back to haunt her and it's funny how every bit of trauma Angela has endured in her past, from living with Dad to diving in the Dixie Lounge, feels easier than the question mark of this current moment. But the past is written, its details known. The future, however, rotted fingers closing off her windpipe, is a jagged cliff overlooking endless possibility.

Her feet are constantly on the edge there, always wobbling.

Angela digs down deep and finds survival. Instinct that ignites with a punch to the squalid face of a million nightmares, knuckles mashing the one bulbous eye that remains intact. The grip on Angela's neck loosens, air spilling into her windpipe, and the only man she ever hated lets loose an oink that goes pinballing around her head.

Angela falls toward the plywood boards, time only to brace for the explosion that never comes. Then she's scrambling along and thinking, *Diagonal*, which is the route she takes to the nearest stairs, climbing, dodging rusted nails glued upturned to the risers.

Rake's way of dissuading company.

A series of gruff oinks follow her up with increased fervor as she approaches the final landing. Angela imagines flat snouts puffing, searching out food, suspecting it's fear these pigs eat.

She expects to find them chowing down at a trough, but instead an orange glow slices the dark and reveals something else: that same damaged and disgusting face, oinks emanating from inside the gaping hole in its center.

The man she used to call Dad isn't going to leave without a fight.

"I killed you once," Angela whispers.

"It was always just a matter of time," he says, words coming not from the mouth he doesn't have, but through the hole in his head, in a swirl of those oinks. He extends his arms to embrace her arrival on the final landing and a chuff of smoke breaks across her face, gets her coughing, hives blooming across her bandaged cheek.

Behind him, rooftop access is visible. An EXIT sign broken in half so only the last two letters remain: IT.

She feels hands on the back of her head and brushes them away like buzzing flies. Gentle caresses find her anyway. A connoisseur's hand roving her battered skull, clucking to appreciate all the trauma she's got stuffed inside.

Burrowing fingers pull back flaps of her skin and the hard shell of her skull somehow folds with it, exposing the wrinkles of her brain to stale cigar smoke.

The Steinmann creaks with elation because at last Angela's tortured thoughts are laid bare in full.

2

ROUGH NIGHT, ISN'T IT?

All of Florida's talking about the baaaad storm bearing down. The neighborhood's scrambling. Put away the patio furniture, kiss your petunia garden goodbye, forget about school for a few days and hope it's still standing when the clouds clear.

Whole state's about to be underwater.

It's not so bad, though. That's what most people around you say. Hunker down for a few days. Gather at the kitchen table, spin the wheel of Life. Play some Go Fish by candlelight. Time slows to a crawl so there's nothing to do except get to know the people you really don't want to get to know.

Your heart's pounding as you watch the man called Dad put the hurricane boards up over the living room windows. Shadows come alive in your house, oily things that might swallow you whole. I mean, your heart is pounding a million miles a minute because you know how bad it's going to get with him inside.

In the dark.

The rain starts early and by the afternoon it's a downpour. Water's pelting off the hurricane boards like ghosts are knocking and there's already fifteen cans of Schlitz on the table. The man called Dad says they're his "fallen soldiers" and he chuckles each time he polishes one of them off, only to crack another within seconds.

Nothing to do but drink the storm under the table.

Except you're wound tighter than a drum 'cause you know it's all going to snap. At some point, the man called Dad will get the urge. He'll start looking at you like you're the reason he's miserable. And maybe you are, but that's not your fault.

Then he'll take it out on Mom.

And those sounds . . . the ones you're going to hear when there's just a few walls between you and their bedroom? You can practically feel them now. The Steinmann conjures them out of thin air and they haunt the stairwell while you stand there, swaying back and forth like a mannequin in a hurricane breeze.

A little slice of home all the way uptown.

You're thinking about how you're ready for the storm. Sixteen years old, ninety-six pounds, but a better shot than those Polk City yokels who go out hunting hog. The man you call Dad took you out there once but you learned more about shotgunning cans of Dixie than how to shoot shotguns.

Your pal Iguana—he got that nickname on account of licking his food before eating it—took you under his wing. To the range. Your life every day after school for six months. It got awkward because he was sure you were taking an interest in him and you shuddered at that thought. Of his tongue flicking your body the way it flicks a Twinkie. Gross. You decided it was best if you were straight with him. "I just want to learn how to shoot," you said. "Be prepared. Just in case."

A lie of omission. Close enough.

Between your father's arsenal and the weapons at Iguana's place, all of them shared freely between he and his own dad, who he called "Pop" with genuine affection that made you jealous, there's one gun in common. A Ruger Mini 14. A hunter's rifle with that classic brown stock. That's the one you want to learn how to shoot.

Iguana told you it was a real nice one and you grinned as you lifted it. Adjusted your stance to accommodate its weight. He told you it does the same damage as an assault rifle. Said you didn't have to worry about that since you were just learning.

Yeah, you remember thinking. *Sure.*

Now the wind's tearing through the abandoned streets, making the hurricane boards wobble, and since the power's out, you can easily hear someone down the road yelling about gators crawling through someone's back yard.

"Aw, Christ," the man you call Dad says.

You assure him it's okay, and it's you who goes into the other room and takes the Ruger down off the wall. He eyes you with a certain suspicion, a sardonic smile slow to spread as he watches you load the magazine. He never suspects a thing because he never believes for a moment you could kill a crab louse.

Let him believe that.

There are parts of the world where it's totally fine for a teenager to sit in the living room with a rifle between her knees, reading old issues of *Circus*. Florida is one of those places.

The man you call Dad is long blitzed and you can tell when the urge takes over by the way he stands up. The kind of force that makes the chair scrape along the floor. You can feel his eyes on the back of your head and you'd give anything not to have to turn around, but his stare carries a certain weight and when you glance over your shoulder, he's leering at you from the shadows.

Thinking bad shit, tongue pursed like Iguana's.

Your hand falls on the rifle, but you know it's going to be hard to get it aimed in the time you've got should he decide to—

He doesn't. He's slinking down the hall, grumbling, "June." His words are mushier than his thoughts. Mom groans to consciousness from her bedroom because she's spent the whole day knowing this was coming.

"I don't feel good," she tries to say but the man you call Dad doesn't care.

"We don't have anything to eat in this house." The next sound is his belt being torn through the loops of his pants, and then a whip crack as he gets ready to blame his wife for whatever inconvenience has crossed his mind.

The gun's in your hands and you're walking, just like Iguana showed you. Just like you trained for. You're tired of those sounds and your mind's been made up for weeks.

You're in the doorway, looking at Mom curled up as the belt cracks down on her again and again. Sometimes, people don't fight. They've got too much to lose, or they've been pummeled into submission by a million bad hands.

The *why* doesn't matter. It's on you now.

You fire a shot and the man you call Dad's back explodes into gore. He turns and you see his exaggerated face, gape-mouthed, rage spiraling around inside his eyes.

Good. That gives you something to shoot at.

The next bullet takes away his face. His skull crumples like a hollow chocolate Easter bunny. The body drops to the foot of the bed and Mom isn't even shrieking. She's looking at you with relief, mutual satisfaction coursing through your bodies.

You tell her now's the time. That you've got a few days to get the story straight. Make this body disappear. Who wouldn't believe he got drunk, heard all the commotion about gators in the neighborhood, and went for a walk? We tried to stop him but that's just how he is, once his mind's made up . . .

Oh yeah, it's going to work.

You wander back to the couch and resume flipping through the magazine while Mom drags the body into the bathroom and gets right to cleaning up. The first thing to go are those beer cans.

You never even had to ask. Neither of you shed a single tear. He wasn't worth one. But you're a murderer now and everything's different.

In a few years, you leave. Make for the city and start a new life trying to help families like yours. Like the man you met on the third floor, who had the same kind of menace as the man you called Dad, but who had apparently recognized it and tried to fight the darkness off.

The fight is what makes us human. Sometimes it's enough to try. Validation for your worldview. People are good. Can change. Even Leo's thinking about trading in his gun if you can believe that.

But not everybody changes. You don't.

You've always been a fighter.

That's what makes you so interesting.

3

RAKE DOES NOT FOLLOW ANGELA upstairs. If that cunt is going to run for the roof, he'll blow the whole fucking thing into outer space.

Only that isn't a god talking, is it? Sounds more like a pathetic wretch of a man.

"Fuck you." Rake grunts like a dog and this confirms the hotel's assessment.

The Steinmann does not care for this development. It feels betrayed by the man it has nested and loved.

Rake gets up off his knees and tries to shake the daze away, realizing he doesn't feel any pain. He's numb from the damage dealt to his body. The embarrassment of it all. His payback is gonna be biblical.

To him, that's who he is now. The Steinmann might consider him a man, but that's a narrow way of looking at things. Another is, up here, Rake walks among gods.

Or devils.

He wipes blood from his mouth, but it keeps on pouring as he wobbles into 2420, past the bathroom floor where that animal Georgie continues to huff down his nearly depleted brick, and he looks so much worse than he had even a few minutes ago.

Georgie's septum has become perforated, and the cocaine is little more than a puddle of powdered blood. Realizing there's nothing left to snort, he grunts his displeasure, glowing eyes flicking toward the door, clocking Rake as he moves to the dresser and grabs the claymore firing device sitting atop it.

"Click three times," Rake says, recalling the instructions. "Ya-bang." The blasting cap wire runs up through the wall into the stair-well next door and continues to the roof.

The plan as he sees it now is: Blow that bitch to high hell, drag Georgie out by the hair and deliver his ass to the lobby of the *Times*. Whether he's dead barely matters. Bastard's more narcotic than man, and with the brain damage to prove it.

The mayor's son as a cautionary tale. The privilege to snort so much junk you can make yourself into a mongoloid. If it can happen to him—

Widespread panic is gonna follow. Blood Thunder has been doing its thing for so long that everyone in the city knows someone who got a bad dose. Sad stories have been circulating for a year, and those whispers are about to become screams.

It's a spiral, after all.

Rake stares at the ceiling with the claymore firing device in his fist. *Click it*, he thinks. But he knows he can't. Not until his couriers ar-rive—t-minus sixty minutes and counting—to clean this place out.

"Okay, okay," Rake says, addressing the hotel he can feel rum-maging through his mind, leaving little stings of cold up there like he's had too much ice cream. "You ain't into this, are you? I hear that."

The Steinmann does not beg. It turns down urges while dialing others up—like a radio knob. That's what the hotel does and, sud-denly, Rake remembers how much more fun life had been before his stay. How satisfying it is to beat the life out of a body with a couple of hammer swings, cracking and reshaping, forging new lifeforms, sculptures of skin and bone. His big idea then had been a gallery ex-hibit in the meatpacking district, one night only, of course, because people would freak when they walked in and saw what he'd been working on, human lives pinned up like portraits. They'd never for-get.

You never were small time, man.

"Why did I give that up?" Rake asks. The sincerity of his tone surprises him and he's at a total loss to answer. For years, he perfected his art and that's what power used to mean to him. Before the Burnt

Book got inside his head, got him "thinking bigger."

Rake glimpses himself over in the hotel room mirror. The blood spilling from his nose oxidized and is closer to mud now. Something about the way it coats his face suggests Vietnam camouflage, and why not. He is at war.

Except, the tie he once had around his neck is gone, must've come loose in his struggle with that bitch, and now he's mesmerized because there's a patch of skin on his neck absorbing every drop of blood that touches it.

A scabrous wound like a pursed mouth, slurping the gore as if it's sipping overspilled coffee off a cup topper.

Rake touches the lesion in disbelief and the hole widens to accommodate the girth of his fingertip. The inside is lubed with pus that allows him to slide in up to his knuckle and Rake knows the living track marks on Sassoon's arms had disquieted him at least in part because of this.

The injury he tried to hide beneath a necktie knot.

He doesn't remember where this came from. His brain's a jumble because the Steinmann's still dialing certain things up, others down. Thoughts as fragments he cannot reconcile, different realities competing. Even as he slides his finger free and watches the infected slime drip off like donut custard . . .

"Show me the truth," Rake says. "From one god to another. You own me that."

"You got it, baby." The answer is spoken by the wound on this throat, which widens into a sort of smile, a second mouth, this one with streams of pus spilling from the corners, dribbling down his bare chest.

He remembers throwing some girl into the tub up here, cracking her skull with his favorite hammer. Catharsis in those sticky wet mallet smacks. Blood finding new orifices to spill through.

She should've been dead. He'd been hard at work on that sculpture for a long time, a full day at least. This was early in his stay, though, and the Steinmann hadn't yet known what to make of him. Maybe it allowed the girl to cling to life for a while longer. Just to see what would happen.

Rake had gone into the next room to consider on which wall to display this piece. A trial run for his gallery idea. That's when she snuck the ice pick into her hand—a tool he often used to shift broken bone fragments around beneath the skin. Give the face some hard angles. And once she had the weapon, she lay still, suffering bash after bash, waiting for the right moment.

It came when Rake thought there was somebody standing in the hall outside the bathroom. A little flicker on behalf of the hotel, nudging things along to keep it interesting. He turned to look and—

Bullseye. Stab to the throat. Back-alley tracheotomy.

The night he died.

Of course, the amount of effort it took to counterattack had sapped the girl of what little life she had stored up, dying in an instant, slumped over the side of the tub, a slow trickle of lifeblood falling as if in mourning.

As for Rake, the sleep that followed was cold and long, and when he awoke, he felt reborn, with a body stronger than before, a brain sharper than ever. He covered his stab wound because there was no explanation for his survival and the only way he could get past it was to set it out of sight, out of mind.

He started to like the tie, told himself it was a *fuck you* to The Man. And it was. Both things could be true.

Now that he remembers, he supposes the only thing that matters to him is that he becomes very important by any means necessary.

The hotel would like him to know he is very important, but this kind of anonymous affection isn't what Rake is after. Every artist wants to live forever in the minds of a public that admires him.

He places the detonator back on the dresser and while there isn't time to get his favorite hammer, he finds himself thinking of the bitch who decked him. How he wouldn't mind using his hands on her. One last sculpture.

There is, after all, some time to kill.

For old time's sake, the hotel suggests, sort of relieved it has succeeded in this distraction, but what the hotel doesn't know is that even before Rake's thoughts were swayed, he'd already decided.

4

ANGELA SPRINTS ACROSS THE ROOFTOP, zigzagging around the assembly of claymores positioned there, the words FRONT TOWARD ENEMY racing by as she widens her gait to avoid going to pieces.

Around her, New York is gone, replaced by skies of oblivion without stars, without Times Square, or anything at all to suggest this is unfolding in the heart of the busiest city on Earth. Her skittering footsteps on gravel echo through the cavernous darkness that hasn't just consumed the world but annihilated it.

The thing she called Dad is now a line on the horizon, blocking her path at the edge of everything. Even from this vantage, his one good eye is popped wider than any eye can go. The only feature left on his face, working three times as hard to illustrate his hatred.

Angela slides to a halt and her shoes leave crooked trails in the gravel. The thing she called Dad staggers forward, dragging the shadows of hell along with him because light doesn't shine on this rooftop.

Unless you've brought some with you.

"You're nothing," Angela screams in defiance because she's grown so much stronger than his memory. Doesn't need a rifle this time. "A weak man. A forgotten ghost. You're shit! That's all you ever were."

This is something the Steinmann does not understand. For all its power and tricks, it cannot prey on the fear of someone who's already conquered theirs.

Angela tightens her brass hand and steadies her nerves. If it has to be violence, it's going to be even quicker this time. She aims again for his one good eye, winding back, about to charge. The thing she called Dad squeals in delight as she tightens into a fighting stance. His feet have somehow become hooves, and he wobbles because balance is a difficult thing to strike in his newly imagined form.

"Mom remarried, you know," Angela says because she's intuited it might hurt this thing she called Dad more than any punch. And it does, because the thing growls in response as she continues, "He's a nice man and they visit every few months. We have tickets to *Cats* . . . not bad for a bunch of '*rootless cosmopolitan assholes*,' right? We're happy now, and the only time we think of you is to remember when we weren't."

The thing she called Dad shrieks in response and his hands bolt outward like an old movie monster, its fingers arched in anticipation, ready to grab her again.

"Nobody thinks of you anymore," Angela says, watching the creature's body slouch, becoming weaker with every insult. Her heart races as she stands her ground, finding a peculiar strength in this defense, dispelling every ounce of hatred she's ever harbored because trauma's an anchor that keeps you in the reeds.

The thing she called Dad staggers into a pocket of shadows that swallows him whole. He simply stays gone. Vanquished by the daughter who will liberate herself time and time again. Whatever it takes.

Maybe the Steinmann cannot conquer her. But Rake can. Angela doesn't realize he's stumbled through the stairwell door at her back. She doesn't hear him, even once the rooftop gravel begins to scuffle.

She's busy with her own triumph, flooded with relief because she's beyond her demons now. Always running from that murder, never confronting it, so certain it might come back to hurt her.

The first bullet glides past her ear and though she never hears the shot in the riled wind, she feels its whoosh pass by.

Angela turns to see Rake coming. Hand outstretched, pistol seemingly dragging him along. It spits at her again, but Angela has already thrown herself to the ground and the bullet flies off into the abyss.

Then she's crawling, stumbling, now running, trying to get wide and clear—even as there's nowhere to go.

Rake's laughter kicks up into the wind and that haunted sound is suddenly everywhere. Booming, disembodied cruelty.

He aims for her heart because it's easier to hit and he still wants the pleasure of breaking and rearranging her face. Except his next shot is still too wide and he's getting impatient, firing again and going even wider. Getting sloppy.

Angela's sure she can drain that gun of all six shots and then rush him because nothing's stopping her from getting off this roof. The man she called Dad couldn't do it, and this punk doesn't stand a chance.

Rake doesn't get to fire again. The claymore ten feet behind him, directly in line with the access door, explodes and the hail of pellets expelled outward from the device sweeps him aside in a sudden storm of shrapnel and flame—the mining equivalent of a sawed-off shotgun flash.

Airborne fragments catch him in the back, cleaving through bone and embedding in his heart. His right leg is blown clean off his body and he tumbles and rolls and comes to a stop on his back, and if Leo were here he would note that same crystalized surprise every punk wears at the end because nobody ever thinks their luck's about to run out.

The mine has a secondary blast radius that catches Angela. Errant shrapnel knocks her off her feet, slices open her face and leaves deep gashes along one side of her torso as her breaths become tired wheezes.

Now she's groaning, the only kind of pep talk she can muster as she crawls toward the stairwell, and her vision's barely there and she doesn't see the figure bundled in errant bone that's waiting just inside.

Certainly doesn't notice the bloodstained razor blade tucked into its skeletal hand, either.

FEAR CITY

1

WHAT RAKE NEVER COUNTED ON is that one floor below, Georgie experienced a moment of clarity right at the end. He overheard Rake say the very thing that would inspire his demise:

"Click three times. Ya-bang."

All Georgie had to do was crawl out of the bathroom and with every last bit of life inside his wasted, poisoned body, pull himself up the length of the dresser, hand stretched toward that detonator device.

Click, click, click.

Ya-bang.

Thunder seemed to bring the hotel down around itself, plaster haze so thick Georgie spilled over in a coughing storm, laughing hysterically on a sheetrock high, imagining Rake blown to pieces and never knowing who had done it. Georgie knows. That's good enough. No endings are perfect.

He died immediately, heart finally surrendering to the chemicals that had rotted every inch of his innards. But even after he was gone, his triumphant laughter stayed behind, prospering inside the halls of the Steinmann, echoing in memorium.

2

RUBEN IS HOLED UP INSIDE the room on ten where Angela had proposed to him her big escape plan. Get the ladder. Climb across. He didn't want to come back up here, but it was the only route the hotel allowed him to take after barely managing to escape the stairwell. He fled back up, body dripping in tar that had come splattering out of those mannequins as he hacked them into plastic firewood.

The Steinmann as a spider egging Ruben the Fly deeper into its twisted web.

He pushed every bit of décor inside the room against the open doorway that Angela had cut through. One desperate way to prevent the endless swarm of department store nightmares from following him in, though he still catches glimpses of their indifferent expressions beyond his makeshift barricade, glowing eyes without life. Hollow fingers tapping with the impatience their expressions refuse to show.

It's only a matter of time before they get in. The furniture blockade contracts like exhaling lungs as they gather the strength to bust all the way through.

"Okay," Ruben sighs, arms afire with heart attack pains. "None of you creepy bastards get to kill me." His body is spent, begging for respite while his spirit can only offer the same pep talk it always does.

You have to stay alive, have to get out . . .

His spirit's as tired as the rest of him. Oddly, it's Leo who keeps him going. The vigilante as his own personal grim reaper, a warning to keep on heeding Papá's advice—fly straight or die bad.

He's seen firsthand how pain and bloodshed devoured Leo's humanity and forged a man so cold there's no path down off that icy mountain. One final lesson because Papá can talk but sometimes the words don't sink in until you see them realized.

Ruben glances out the window where a cleaning person in the office across the way, but one floor beneath, is emptying a trash can tucked under a desk in a corner office.

"Angela," Ruben says, taken by a new hope as he uses the axe head to crack the Steinmann's window apart, glass shards raining down around his feet like diamonds. "You were almost right." He shouts across the alleyway until his throat goes hoarse. No use. Skyscraper glass is reinforced and the custodian inside is none the wiser.

So he does the only other thing that comes to mind—winds his arm back and hurls that axe across the alley like a boomerang.

In a stroke of luck, the blade strikes the window head-on and wedges itself there. The spidering glass catches the attention of one very startled custodial worker, whose jaw is on the floor as she inches toward it, staring in disbelief.

"Now look at me!" Ruben screams, waving his arms back and forth in the shattered window space, cheering when the custodian does in fact look up and catch his gaze, and now Ruben's whooping because something goes right for once, and the monsters behind him cease trying to enter. He looks back and they're just standing motionless, as if they've lost the will to fight.

Ruben puts a thumb to his ear and a pinkie to his mouth in a telephone gesture and the custodian nods with such pronouncement he sees it from here, and then he's applauding as she runs hurriedly to the desk phone and picks it up, placing an outgoing call.

That's when he starts to cry because Ruben knows he's going to make it home.

3

SHADOWS DANCE AROUND LEO LIKE scarecrows in a summer breeze. Pointless deterrents. The Steinmann unable to help itself.

On twenty-one, he picks up the trail ignited by Angela's blood-stained hand bandages and the little patters on the floor he realizes are intended to lead him the rest of the way. He follows them exact, intuiting he cannot afford to make one wrong step.

Ya-bang.

On twenty-three, there's the risk of missing the tripwire waiting for him inside of Rake's vestibule room. That eager shotgun attached to the wall like a sentry, waiting to decapitate any trespassers.

Leo's guard is perpetually heightened through years of caution—the only reason he's still alive.

The room he climbs into is 2408 and it's built on Blood Thunder. Bricks of the stuff stacked to the ceiling. A warehouse of poison. At last he's reached the belly of the beast. He's tempted to burn it all with a couple flicks from the BIC on the dresser, but the chemical haze that would enflame this space would kill him and anyone else still up here.

Everything on twenty-four is cast in a gauzy overlay and the world smells of fire. The air, acrid and unpleasant. Leo taps his thigh as he walks, wondering if he hasn't made a mistake in discarding his weapon, fearing he's too late. That he missed the war and a victor has been decided without him.

Georgie's laughter croons. A haunted birdsong Leo interprets as mockery, though the hotel is going to have to try a little harder to spook him after all the visions and bloodshed it's forced him to suffer.

He's where the hall splits into the wings of a T and there's motion on his left. A figure lurching out of the stairwell through a fleeting cloud of plaster and smoke. Angela with a blade sticking out of her shoulder, wobbling there, embedded.

"Y-y-you, uh . . ." she stutters, eyes barely recognizing him, "found me." Her forearm goes up along the wall to steady herself.

Leo moves toward her but stops quick when he spots a bigger shadow cutting through the gauze. That familiar skeletal arm reaching for her, fingers wiggling, brushing aside Angela's mottled hair, eager to take possession of her bones.

She doesn't notice. Her lips are moving but Georgie's sustained laughter is booming so loud it drowns her words.

The creature glides into the hall, coat flapping behind it, allowing Leo another look at its physiology: bones fused to other bones. A monstrosity the hotel seems to have hastily assembled and then stuffed inside a jet-black trench coat.

Its outstretched hand has six fingers, each one closing around the knife handle, which is when Angela comes alive again, as if through a surge of electricity—ten thousand volts straight to her heart. She reacts to the blade as it's plunged further down inside her, crying out and dropping to her knees, falling to her stomach.

Georgie's laugh suggests he's enjoying this clumsy pratfall and Leo charges, hand falling on the creature's coated sleeve, pulling it back, away from Angela. The forearm snaps off, falling out of the coat and shattering across the floor.

Now he's got the monster's attention.

It turns to face him as Georgie's disembodied laugh roars at its most deafening volume yet, distorted as if piped through a dozen broken boomboxes.

Leo stares into the face he cannot describe. It's everything and nothing. Monstrous, yet vacant. It makes him hope for the end.

He deserves it.

Only the Steinmann feels different. It does not understand how Leo has resisted his own despair and perhaps it was wrong to allow

Rake to experience such a fiery demise. Leo is not coming along quietly.

The eyes beneath the brim of the creature's hat are multiple, a scramble of arachnid eyes, each bulb alive with the blight and suffering that defines human existence. Starving people dying alone in obscurity, diseases that devour loved ones, accidents that bring untimely ends without rhyme or reason.

It's the sixty-year-old man who works right up until retirement only to be shot by a mugger on his way home on the eve of his freedom. The small girl whose innocence is taken away by a classroom of bullies, cruelty that carves a lifetime of trauma into the contours of her soul. The gay man who must live in secret, struggling to process the virus wasting his lover to nothing while the uncaring world he's going to be left behind in suggests it's his fault for the way he was born.

The Bonefreek's face is all these things and much worse. To Leo, it's like looking into a mirror and seeing the last decade reflected. All he can muster is a tired laugh because he has nothing else to give.

It's his laugh that hurts the creature. His aggravated dismissal of the Bonefreek. His arms shoot out with his palms overturned and he asks, "What more could you possibly do to me?"

Leo recognizes himself inside the creature's face and it's suddenly clear, as if he's looking at himself twenty or thirty years from now—after he's dead and buried, flesh rotted away to reveal the monster underneath.

They're one in the same. Rivermen, both. Monsters who force the unwilling onto the boat. Their weapons—be it blades or Barettas—the paddles that carry souls to the other side. To the only world Leo knows anymore. A place of gunpowder ghosts and graffiti tombs.

The creature recoils away from the vigilante, feeling like a neutered dog, and the purr in its throat reignites upon the sight of Angela writhing around on the floor, choking on the blood spilling from her mouth.

"I told you . . . she's mine." Leo bends to help Angela to her feet and the Bonefreek glides back, stunned by this defiance. It feels weak in this moment, its one remaining forearm shielding itself from further resistance.

Angela crashes against Leo, groaning into his shoulder. Her face is loose, eyes on the cusp of checking out. She tries to smile and more blood pours past her lips, extending a red grin all the way to her cheeks.

When Leo looks up, the Bonefreek is gone. He drags Angela with graceless motion, telling her, "Keep it together."

"How long does a human body sit in a gator's stomach?" Her question is soft and airy and doesn't seem to be pointed at Leo. Nevertheless, it offers a window into her mind that roils his curiosity and makes him glad he found her.

"That cup of coffee is the only thing keeping us alive right now," he says because he cannot lose her and risk widening the spiral. Families across the city suffering, their cases slapped onto the desks of other, already overworked agents. Less attention, more neglect. The stuff of nightmares.

They're moving past 2408 when a draft of bitter cold strikes out, a vacuum current somehow pulling them toward the black maw of the room. Angela is launched off her feet, her body going horizontal, hovering in space like some magician's assistant, and then disappearing into the gloom, abruptly swallowed by the flow. The Steinmann as a tantruming child, flipping the game board over.

Angela spills across the hotel room floor, bouncing like a tumbleweed, screaming as she's pulled right toward the hole in the ground: Rake's secret passage. She falls straight through, the world alternating in flashes of black and white as her head bounces off ladder rungs all the way down.

Leo is caught in the same current. His face smashes on the carpet. Rug burns along his chin as he glides toward the same latch that swallowed Angela, bricks of Blood Thunder sucked down into the black ahead of him. And then he's overboard too, careening headfirst into that pile of unbroken cocaine waiting to receive him.

Angela's buried beneath that junk. She breaks Leo's fall with a grunt, breathless because she's already got air wheezing out one side of her punctured body. Doesn't even feel the embedded shrapnel slowly killing her as she lifts her arm up through the pile where Leo interlocks with her fingers and pulls her out. Two damaged bodies groaning in miserable concert.

"We have to keep going," he says, breathless, resuming their conjoined hobble toward the exit. Leo's eyes on that fatal tripwire.

It's where the Bonefreek is waiting, body like a flapping black curtain before the rest of its shape takes form, and then it glides from the shadows, its remaining arm swinging up and somehow reaching halfway across the room—length like a pterodactyl's wingspan. In its fist, a hungry straight razor.

Leo helps Angela over the tripwire. She coughs and staggers, the internal bleeding in her brain reducing her to a creature of instinct, and just barely one of those. He tries to follow and catches a slash from the blade as it comes falling down, tearing a gash through his shoulder.

The force of this attack gets Leo turning halfway around and the old man's still got reflexes. His hands shoot up over his face as the freek readies another slash. Leo catches the oversized hand in his own, and with a tug worth all his weight, yanks the monster forward so its skeletal ankles snap the tripwire.

Buckshot turns the freek's coat into ribbons. All that's left of it is a pile of anarchic bones stacked beneath a coil of swirling gun smoke.

"Elevator," Leo says, but Angela is way of head of him, limping into the hall without hearing anything he has to say.

Leo catches himself in the mirror as he's moving past and the one reflection there is to be expected: Leo with the Baretta to his head, only this time—

His boot sails through the glass because nobody else is dying today. And then he's crunching over seven years bad lack beneath his feet, unmoved because he's already had a decade's worth and counting.

One errant brick of Rake's poison sits beside the doorway. Leo tucks it under his arm because he needs people to understand what's killing the city. Being a good citizen was always beyond the scope of his abilities. So much easier to point and shoot. That feels laughably short-sighted now.

Angela is halfway to the elevator, leaning on the wall, shoulder inching down like she's ready to throw in the towel. Isn't going to make it any further. And with half the city on strike, there's no guarantee an ambulance will reach her in time.

He's going to have to improvise.

"Let's go," Leo says, hooking her arm around his neck and dragging her the rest of the way. "Too close to quit now." She's conscious enough to tap the down button while mumbling something about hurricane boards he doesn't understand.

The doors slide open and Angela goes tumbling into the car with Leo following.

He taps 2F, which is as low as the north elevator will descend, but the doors remain open. Stuck, or because the Steinmann does not appreciate this turn of events.

"It's not going to let us leave," Angela says with surprising urgency and cognizance, given her injuries. Her voice a slurry cocktail of hysteria and fear while her eyes dance with nervous fire. "It's never going to let us go."

But then the doors close and the elevator begins grinding its way down and relief lasts as long as a single breath and then the lights inside click off, prompting Angela to whimper because her fears have been confirmed. There is no way she'll see the city sidewalk again because she feels the Bonefreek rising out of the onyx behind her, the familiar glint of its straight razor in her peripheral, shining like a star overhead.

Frenzy makes Angela vulnerable because death is the great equalizer. Maybe she did vanquish her fears in this place, but the end is something else. Everyone fears the black because you only die once and there's no way to practice or prepare for it. As such, nobody really dies with dignity. Why should she be any different?

Leo wedges himself between Angela and the freek and turns his back on the creature. It has no power over him. He takes Angela by the shoulders and offers his most compassionate face. "It has to be this way," he says. "Please understand."

He doesn't wait for an answer—she's too dazed to give him one anyway—just closes his hands around her neck and squeezes her throat.

Angela doesn't expect this. Her face ignites in surprise and her meager resistance makes Leo squeeze harder. She starts to beg but the best she can do is grunt, her pleas never materializing as words.

"I have to," he says through gritted teeth, attempting to convince himself as much as her, but strangulation takes forever and it's agony to watch the confusion in her eyes, even as they soften into grim acceptance.

He keeps squeezing until Angela is good and dead, her body dangling in his hands like an empty suit. Then he guides her down to the floor and releases her neck in order to cross himself. And then she's slumped there, arm draped over Leo's boot. He kicks it away and turns to face an otherwise empty car.

The Bonefreek is nowhere to be found.

He's alone with Angela.

"I beat you," he tells the Steinmann, and then rides all the way down.

4

HE GETS THERE BEFORE HE gets there.

It isn't the Steinmann's front desk, but it is a front desk. Leo looks down at the glass countertop and finds ashen clouds swirling there in lieu of his reflection, and he knows that every stay at this hotel inevitably leads here—to this place on the edge of nothing.

Angela remains curled at his feet, the brick of Blood Thunder beside her. Her eyes as glass marbles, unblinking and haunted. Unlike the shock and disbelief always plastered across the faces of his victims, she wears something a bit closer to peace.

Maybe in the next life, Leo thinks. *Maybe for both of us . . .*

This was not the action of the vigilante. This was not punishment. It was love. The only kind of love a killer is equipped to show, ringing her neck until it's the color of a tomato. The only way to protect her eternal soul.

He's in the business of saving those now, or at least preventing hers from becoming another echo trapped forever in the halls of this miserable hotel.

He kneels to tend to her, to straighten her body and dignify her corpse, one last show of respect for all she's given him. As he bends, he's back in the confines of the elevator with pity in his throat, choking on any words he might offer.

Soft laughter underneath everything. The hotel's mischievous giggle saying, "See what we made you do?"

Only it's the hotel that doesn't see. Leo slips the knife from Angela's shoulder, wiping the blade clean on his shirt as the Steinmann's cackle warps, a sound like a melting mix tape, the airy voice becoming a wobble.

Leo uses the blade to puncture the cocaine and plant a generous mound on Angela's tongue and the hotel isn't laughing anymore. The giggle has become an impotent scream as Leo forces Angela's mouth closed, jimmying her head around to get enough of it down her throat, inside her body.

"Come on," he whispers while the surrounding screams crescendo, reaching a pitch that shatters the elevator light. Leo leans forward to shield Angela from falling glass shards that pelt off his back instead of her face. He just stares at the now-dark outline of her face, brushing her forehead and saying, "You have to make it," through gnashed teeth.

He doesn't have to wait long for the adrenaline to work. Her pulse is faint, isn't all the way gone yet, and tiny tremors glide through her face, a slight wrinkle like an ocean wave on her forehead, one twitching eye, a flexing throat that causes her lips to purse as though she's about to vomit.

Angela is reborn through a cocaine high, springing up, launching back to life and shooting to her feet because her legs are rockets and her heart is pumping molten lava that sends her pinballing around the elevator.

The blade that's covered in Blood Thunder clatters and a cloud of epinephrine-cut-blow puffs up around them. Leo has nuked her heart, bought her a new life on Rake's dime.

The dusted junk hardens into a crust on Angela's blood-caked face. She catches sight of herself in the mirror, has to squint through the dark and wait for her eyes to focus, and then she screams at the sight because it looks like she's clawed her way out of hell.

And then Leo stands up to help guide her back down, except he can't because he's out of there. Away from Angela and the elevator, back inside the Nowhere Lobby with bigger things on his mind.

Like the man behind the desk who isn't a man at all, although he is mocked up to resemble one. A plastic, featureless mask creates a face where one does not otherwise exist. A pink doorman's cap sits crooked atop his head.

"I'm the manager," he says, muffled because the mask has no

mouth, "and this has all been a terrible misunderstanding."

Leo has nothing to say because wherever this is, it's not reality. When he glances at his feet, he can see the elevator. Somehow he's there, sitting on the floor, rocking Angela, holding her tight and encouraging her to take deep breaths as the car approaches the second floor.

There, siren songs fill the air and agitated voices are louder the closer they get to the landing.

"To make it up to you," the manager continues, "we are prepared to offer you residence in a suite of rooms on our famous twenty-fourth floor."

You're in the elevator. Almost to the bottom. . .

"No," the manager says, shaking its head because it has access to Leo's thoughts. "I'm afraid you are here. You are checking in."

"I don't want to," Leo says to Angela in the elevator, an air of desperation in his tone. Her brain is still too baked to comprehend anything beyond the impossibility of being alive. The doors open in a hail of flashlight beams that go skittering around as tactical voices bark commands from the dark behind pointed rifles.

"I know her," Leo hears Ruben say from somewhere behind the response team. "She's with me."

And then that scene is gone and life in the Nowhere Lobby is all that's left. The darkness inside of Leo might be a powerful, corrosive thing for the Steinmann, an ever-expanding spiral that collects collateral damage like baseball cards, but there has to be another way out of this.

"I need that coffee," Leo says, hoping Angela's brain works well enough to process the meaning of those words. It's all been shit for so long, he needs the change. More than that, he wants it.

The darkness around the desk recedes, bands of white light cracking through the starry gloom, flooding in and sweeping through, gobbling up large swaths of oblivion, forcing what little of it remains to exist on the periphery.

Cleansing light because the opposite of fear is knowledge and understanding.

Leo forces himself to stare, squinting against the searing pain the light brings, insurmountable heat on his eyeballs. He holds his ground because, beneath the pain, something else is occurring.

Parts of him long dead are waking up, the spiral slowing.

"Sir," the manager says with a stitch of panic, "if you'll just agree to our terms, you will find a very pleasant stay."

This as the surrounding light builds to a crescendo. A single flash closer to a nuclear blast and the manager cries out because it's too late. He's annihilated and the world is forever changed. The energy has shifted.

Leo's looking at rows of stainless cabinet doors, each of them popping open, steel gurneys sliding out like metal tongues.

They're all empty, save for one on the far end where Louis Robert Tommlinson lies in the cold flesh because his soul's long gone. Puncture wounds across his chest and stomach, every drop of blood long expelled.

Nobody escapes the spiral.

The tag dangling off his wrist is dated September 10, 1980.

He's been dead for three and a half years.

There was no better world, his death didn't make the slightest difference. It's as when Leo shot him in the head deep within the bowels of the netherworld where the hotel had stashed him. Louis Robert Tommlinson no longer matters to anyone. He did his damage long ago, ensnaring Leo in the spiral.

Now the ride is stopping. Leo is getting off.

Louis Robert Tommlinson opens his eyes and sits up, the lines of his face regenerating. He notices Leo and though he doesn't seem to understand how this is possible, there is a flicker of recognition.

"You found me, man," he says.

"I did."

"It's cold."

Leo nods but doesn't agree. He's warm all the way to his toes.

Leo doesn't know if there's a road back, or if that matters. All those futures he had a hand in harming, those the hotel had delighted in showing him—and the many more it did not—are still out there, broken and suffering for things Leo has done.

But the knowledge has not destroyed him as intended.

The dead man hops off the slab, hot stepping across the floor because the cold linoleum stings. "Can I come with you?"

Leo's in the doorway, looking up from the bowels of the morgue, realizing he's been here, inside this hell, for a decade. At the very top of the stairs, though, light is beginning to spill through.

The dead man extends an arm in a desperate stretch and the punctured swastika over his heart is oozing blood he doesn't have and his eyes go wide with terror in the second before his body is reclaimed

GRAFFITI TOMBS

by the shadows. "Please," he says, and then his arm slips into the darkness with the rest of him and he's gone.

A fate worse than any Leo could've given.

Some men never get beyond the dark.

And then Leo's ascending the stairs, climbing toward the light. Leaving this place behind.

BIO

Matt Serafini is a screenwriter and the author of *Rites of Extinction, Under the Blade, Island Red, Feral,* and *Devil's Row.* His non-fiction has appeared in the pages of *Fangoria, Scream,* and *HorrorHound.* Matt lives in New England with his family, where he spends way too much time tracking down obscure slasher movies.

Other Grindhouse Press Titles